GIRL OF THE YEAR™ 2017 ★

GABRIELA

Time for Change

by Varian Johnson

Scholastic Inc.

Published by Scholastic Inc., *Publishers since 1920.* SCHOLASTIC and associated logos are trademarks and/or registered trademarks of Scholastic Inc. The publisher does not have any control over and does not assume any responsibility for author or third-party websites or their content.

This book is a work of fiction. Names, characters, places, and incidents are either the product of the author's imagination or are used fictitiously, and any resemblance to actual persons, living or dead, business establishments, events, or locales is entirely coincidental and not intended by American Girl or Scholastic Inc.

Book design by Angela Jun

Cover photo by Michael Frost for Scholastic

Author photo by Kenneth P. Vail

Special thanks to Martha Chapman.

americangirl.com/service

ISBN 978-1-338-13701-9

10 9 8 7 6 5 4 3 2 1   17 18 19 20 21

Printed in the USA 58 • First printing 2017

*For Elizabeth, Adrienne, Savannah,
and Sydney*

—V.J.

 Contents

Chapter 1

Voices

I leaned forward, my seat belt tugging against me, and peered through the window as Mama steered the car into the Franklin High School parking lot. Daddy looked back at me and Red. "You two ready?" he asked.

"Sure thing, Uncle Rob," Red said, rubbing his hands together. "It's going to be amazing. Like a hot, glazed doughnut on an ice-cold day." Then he pointed to Daddy. "Your turn."

Daddy's eyebrows bunched up on his forehead as he tried to come up with the next line. "Um . . . like a . . . like a . . ." He stopped and shook his head. "Maybe I'll leave the poetry to you and Gabby. You're the experts, not me."

"Want to help your dad out, cuz?" Red asked me.

I closed my eyes. It was easier to see the words that way sometimes. Like I was writing them on an invisible piece of paper in my head. "Like a hot, glazed doughnut on an ice-cold day. Like springtime showers in the month of May."

"Like a single snowflake that lands on your skin," Red said.

"Like . . . like sitting at a campfire with cousin and kin."

Then Red nodded toward Mama. "Want to join in, Aunt Tina?"

Mama laughed as she steered through the parking lot. "How about, like a parking lot full of kids excited about spoken word poetry."

Red laughed as well. "Good example of using your surroundings to flesh out your verses, but we're going to have to work on your form a bit."

The parking lot *was* full of people—mostly high school students and adults—but there were some kids who looked to be in middle school like me and Red, too.

Yesterday afternoon at our Friday meeting, Red had told our poetry group about Voices, a spoken word competition. This poetry slam was for high school students, but there would be another one for middle school kids in just five weeks—and we would be competing! We were checking out the high school slam to get an idea of what to expect for ours.

Voices

"Andy said they'd be parked in the front," Mama said to Daddy. "Can you call him and—"

"There they are!" Red said, pointing.

I whipped my head around. Sure enough, there was Teagan, my best friend, jumping up and down to get our attention. Her grandfather, Mr. Harmon, stood behind her, holding her overnight bag and her humongous backpack.

I rolled down my window. "Teagan!" I yelled, waving at her.

"Gabby!" she yelled back.

"Why are you yelling?" Red asked. "Didn't you just see her yesterday?"

"I'm always happy to see my best friend," I said, elbowing him.

I'd been friends with Teagan ever since her grandpa came on as the art teacher at Liberty Arts Center, the community organization Mama founded. Teagan and I could finish each other's sentences, and we almost always knew what the other was thinking. *She* was as awesome as a hot, glazed doughnut on an ice-cold day.

As soon as Mama parked, I scrambled out of the car and hugged Teagan, almost knocking off her turquoise beanie. Her grin was wide across her freckled face. "I don't

know what I'm more happy about—the competition or the sleepover," she said.

"Me, neither!" I replied. Now that Teagan and I were going to different schools, I had hardly spent any time with her outside of poetry club meetings. But we were going to have a long-overdue sleepover tonight.

There were so many things I needed to catch her up on. Just a couple days ago, I won the election to be a Kelly Middle School Ambassador, one of a group of students who helped make the school better for everyone. But technically, I wasn't the only student who had won. I tied with my mortal enemy, Aaliyah Reade-Johnson. Well, maybe *former* mortal enemy, now . . . *friend*? I wasn't sure yet. But we were being nicer to each other, and we sat together at lunch the other day.

Dad took the bags from Mr. Harmon and placed them in the trunk. "We'll meet you all right here after the competition," he said.

"And stick together," Mama added, before kissing us each on the forehead. Even Teagan. "Text if you need us. We'll be nearby."

We waved good-bye, then made our way toward the school. We could already hear music coming from the auditorium.

"Alejandro, Bria, and Isaiah are inside," Red said, glancing at a text on his phone. "They saved seats for us." He winked. "Just look for their hair."

Red was joking, but he was right—all three of our friends had epic hairdos. I spotted Bria's big, bushy ponytail first, then Alejandro's long black hair. But Isaiah's huge Afro beat them all. It easily made him five inches taller.

Red pointed to the stage. "And look! They've even got a DJ. That's what's up!"

A kid stood behind a table with neon-green headphones over his ears, working two turntables. A few high schoolers danced on the floor in front of the stage, challenging each other to different moves. Who knew that poetry slams were such a party?

We made our way to our friends. Bria and Alejandro waved while Isaiah said, "Good morrow, my ladies" over the music. "You ready to hear today's good word?" Isaiah considered Shakespeare the greatest writer and poet that ever lived and was always channeling his voice.

"Thanks for sss-saving our seats," I said as Teagan and I dropped into chairs beside him. My stutter, which always acted up when my emotions were running high, gave away how excited I was to be here. *My first real poetry slam.*

A few minutes later, a woman came onstage holding a

cordless microphone. Her multicolored dreadlocks were pulled into a ponytail, tied off with a lime-green scarf. She reminded me of our social studies teacher at school, Ms. Tottenham, who always wore cool outfits, too. The DJ faded the music as the auditorium quieted down.

"Ladies and gentlemen, welcome to Voices. My name is Jackie King, and I'll be your emcee. Today we have ten—TEN!—outstanding groups ready to share their dynamic poems. But before we begin, let me hear you make some noise for all our young poets today!"

The auditorium erupted in cheers and applause. I couldn't help but laugh to myself—the party continued even into the competition.

Jackie went on to explain the rules and scoring. The slam was broken into five rounds. Each team had to perform at least one group poem, which could include as few as two or as many as four members of the team. Poets had a three-minute time limit, and props weren't allowed.

That all seemed simple enough. I wondered how Red would break us up for the various rounds. Some ideas for a group piece about our bond as a poetry team were already stirring in my mind.

Jackie introduced the judges next. There was a youngish-looking guy with big glasses, a middle-aged lady with some funky beaded jewelry, and a kid who looked like he was in high school. Red told us yesterday that with these competitions, it's not about "poetry experts" judging your technique. The judges are regular people, like Mama or Mr. Harmon. Spoken word is meant to be accessible to everyone—meaning everyone's opinion is valid, too. I loved that.

"Now, before we get started," Jackie continued, jumping up and down a little, "I'm going to warm you guys up a bit." Her energy was contagious—I was bouncing in my seat a little bit, too. "How many of you have been to a poetry slam before?"

Arms shot up all around us. Red was the only one in our group with his hand in the air.

"Okay, okay—we've got some newbies," she said, surveying the audience. "Well, you guys are in for a treat. Poetry slams are not a spectator sport—you are just as important as the poets. They feed off your energy. Now, we don't like a lot of talking while the poets are onstage, but there are other ways to show some love. So let's practice." She pulled back her sleeves and raised the hand that wasn't holding the mic. "I know everybody out there can clap, but what about snapping your fingers? Can you do that?"

She snapped her fingers and so did we. The noise was like the rain hitting the tin roof of the Liberty theater.

"And what about your feet?" she asked. "They're not just made for walking. Let's see if you can stomp."

We pounded our shoes against the floor. Just for fun, I threw in a shuffle, too. I was pretty new to poetry, but had been dancing—with Mama as one of my teachers—all my life. I took tap, hip-hop, and ballet, but tap had always been my favorite. I knew how to make noise with my feet, that was for sure!

"And can you say mmm-hmm?" she asked, leaning to the side.

"Mmm-hmm!" we said back.

"You got it!" Jackie said. "Feel free to cheer on our poets whenever you're feeling it. I promise, they'll be feeling it, too." She quickly glanced offstage, then nodded and turned back to us. "So, if you're all ready, we're going to kick things off with what we call our Sacrificial Poets. These poets aren't competing today—they are here to set the bar for the judges only—but they still deserve your love, so let's hear it for the Pink Poetics!"

Teagan elbowed me as everyone clapped. "We need to come up with a cool name for our group."

I nodded, wishing I had brought my new poetry

notebook so I could brainstorm ideas. Mama had given me the notebook last night as a congratulations gift for winning the ambassadors election. It said DREAM BIG on the front in silver sparkly letters. I couldn't wait to start filling it up with poetry!

The stage lights shifted from yellow to fuchsia as four girls walked onto the stage. No, not walked—strutted.

They took their places, their hot pink jackets shiny under the lights. One girl stood with her arms crossed, a wicked scowl on her face. Another posed with her back to us and her hands on her hips. A third stood with her fist high in the air. It kind of reminded me of the opening positions for one of my hip-hop routines—some girls mid-pop, others mid-lock, and still others mid-drop. Everyone in the middle of a dance move, frozen in place. Like department store mannequins about to come alive.

The remaining girl moved to the front of the stage. She stared at us for a long time, not saying anything, and for a second, I thought maybe she had forgotten her poem. Then she brought the microphone to her lips, and words exploded from her mouth.

Her voice filled the room, making us all sit back, as she told us a powerful story about women fighting for equality. After a couple lines, she marched from the center of the

stage to the girl with her fist in the air. That poet came alive, too, and joined the first girl in marching. My heart pumped in my chest as their feet hit the floor in unison, their stomps coinciding with their inspiring words.

"We demand to be seen.

We demand to be heard.

We are mighty.

We are many.

You will hear us *roar*!"

That got some "Mmm-hmms" from the audience, including two from Teagan and me.

Then the second girl took over. Unlike the first poet, this girl was quiet, her shoulders slowly rising and falling as she spoke. Was there something wrong with her mic? I leaned in so I could hear better, then peeked at Teagan and Isaiah. They were leaning in, too.

I glanced around. *Everyone* was leaning in. No one moved. It seemed like no one was even breathing. Something Mama told me once popped into my head. When a great dancer puts her whole self into a performance, the audience feeds off that performance as well. Maybe they laugh or maybe people cry—but whatever we as dancers do onstage, we have the power to move them. To make them feel something. I knew what it felt like to put my whole self into a

performance, but I was usually onstage, hardly ever in the audience. I totally got what Mama was saying.

The other two girls were just as awesome, pointing to each other and the audience as they traded off on lines, like two people passing a basketball.

I could tell the poem was almost over when the four girls said a verse in unison. By the time they were done, I was throwing in not only shuffles but stomping toe-heel, toe-heel, like we did in tap class warm-ups. These girls deserved more than regular old stomps!

When they were done, Red leaned forward and caught my gaze. "So what do you think?" he asked me, his toothy grin shining big. "Amazing, right?"

I smiled right back at him. "Yeah. Amazing."

Amazing Voices

Like a hot, glazed doughnut on an ice-cold day
Like springtime showers in the month of May
Like a single snowflake that lands on your skin
Like sitting at a campfire with cousin and kin
Poetry makes you feel—

Time for Change

It's real
The fire, the heat
The words are alive
The cold, the chill
How can you keep still
When the words are flowing
And going
And stirring
Up feelings inside you?
The emotion, it's growing
It wants to burst through
So you let it
And then you worry the amazement is ending
But up comes another verse
And you smile
It's just the beginning

Chapter 2

A Perfect Pair

So, what do you think about calling the poetry group the Liberty Bells?" I asked Teagan later that afternoon. I was sprawled out on my bedroom floor supposedly doing my homework, but all I could think about was those awesome spoken word groups.

The way they used their bodies to strengthen their words—jumping, leaping, twisting, and turning—it was like hip-hop, but without music.

And their names. Pink Poetics. Radical Verses. We *had* to come up with something better than "The Poetry Group."

"Teagan?" I asked again. "Did you hear me?"

"What?" she said. She was at my desk, finishing her own homework. Something for her coding class.

"The Liberty Bells," I repeated, just as my gray-and-white cat, Maya, sauntered into the room.

I got up and walked over to the desk. "Or what about Vibin' and Versin'? Red would probably love that. Or maybe—"

I stopped. Beside Teagan's coding notebook sat what looked like a test. Half the paper was covered in red ink.

"Oh, I'm sorry," I said, turning away from her. "I d-d-didn't realize you were-were . . ."

Teagan quickly placed her notebook over the paper. "No, it's okay. Just going over last week's quiz." She scratched her head, knocking her beanie askew over her strawberry-blonde hair. "I'm not making much progress anyway. I should probably take a break."

Last time I'd talked to Teagan about her new school, she was feeling really overwhelmed. Main Line Tech was one of the best STEM-focused magnet schools in the Philly area, but I hated seeing her so stressed out. "How about this—we take a break for an hour, and then get back to homework? Okay?"

Teagan nodded. "Sorry I had to bring all my books over. I'm just worried I'll fall even more behind if I don't get any work done this weekend." She straightened her beanie. "But you're right. What do you want to do?"

"I know the perfect thing." I opened up my closet, then wheeled out my performance case. The big black trunk was

a gift from Grandma last Christmas and quickly became one of my favorite things. I used it to store my laptop, recording equipment, and dance gear. This summer, Teagan and I made it even cooler by spray-painting my name on it in big white letters. Now, I opened it up, and pulled out my pink-and-purple electronic drum kit.

"Remember how the girl from Pink Poetics kept stomping onstage?" I repeated part of the poem, striking one of the drum pads when the girls had stomped.

"We d-d-d-demand to be seen.
We demand to be heard.
We are mighty.
We are many.
You will hear us *roar*!"

Teagan sat down beside me and tapped on another drum pad with her finger, creating the boom of a bass drum. "You think we should add music to our poems? Is that even allowed?"

I shook my head. "I don't think so, but maybe we could use our bodies like drums, stomping or clapping when we want to emphasize something." I banged on the pads a few times. "You know, instead of just standing there."

"Oh, like the boy from that group, Uni Verse," Teagan said. "He was slapping his legs, all quick and staccato and everything." She tapped the drum pad again, this time with a more complicated rhythm.

"That's a nice beat," I said.

She nodded. "I heard it at school last week. One of the kids in my class wrote a computer program that makes drum sounds when you press certain keys."

"That's so cool," I said. "Is he a friend of yours?"

She stopped tapping the drum. "Kind of. We talk a little in class when we're working on group projects or homework."

"Nice. Maybe he can help us come up with some mad beats for the poetry slam?"

Teagan shrugged, an odd look on her face. "Maybe." She picked up a drumstick and twirled it . . . or tried to. It fell on the floor with a clatter. "Well, that wasn't as easy as I thought it would be." She laughed.

I reached down to grab the stick and started twirling it myself.

"Speaking of not-easy things . . ." Teagan continued, "how's it going with Aaliyah? I can't believe you have to share the Sixth-Grade Ambassador role with her."

This time the drumstick didn't just fall to the floor, it somehow soared across the room, narrowly missing Maya.

A Perfect Pair

Teagan thought they were forcing Aaliyah and me to work together? That wasn't how it happened at all. Maya meowed and ran out of the room as I found my words.

"A-A-A-Actually, it was my idea to sh-sh-share the role with Aaliyah," I said. "Instead of having another election to break the tie."

"Really?" Teagan's face scrunched up. "Even after everything that happened last year?"

We had first met Aaliyah Reade-Johnson in fifth grade. She could be really bossy, and always spoke her mind. And lots of stuff she said came out sounding not very nice, even if she didn't mean it that way. As if that wasn't bad enough, she made fun of my stutter all last year.

But things were different in sixth grade. I learned that behind her prickly exterior, there was someone who used her voice to speak up for people, like when she'd stood up for Isaiah after someone called him a mean name. And she finally apologized for making fun of my stutter.

"Maybe we were wrong about Aaliyah," I said.

Teagan shrugged again. "Maybe. But still, be careful, okay?"

"I will," I said, then busied myself with the drum kit. It didn't seem like the right time to tell Teagan that Aaliyah and I had eaten together at lunch this week, too.

"Hey," I said, eager to change the subject. "M-M-Maybe we should talk about Hallow—Halloween."

Teagan's face lit up. "I have *the best* idea! Wait—" She grabbed my hand. "You *do* want to dress up together this year, right?"

"Of course!" I said. "Just because we aren't at the same school doesn't mean we can't trick-or-treat together!" Teagan and I had dressed up as a pair every Halloween we'd known each other. One year, we borrowed one of her grandpa's old shirts and were conjoined twins. It was kind of hard walking around the neighborhood like that, and we fell down probably a thousand times, but it was super fun.

"So what do you think we should be?" I asked. "Zombie princesses? Roller derby girls?"

She twirled a piece of hair around her finger. "What about . . . a social butterfly?"

I frowned. "You mean like someone who has a bunch of friends? How is that even a costume?"

"No, silly," she said. "I mean, yeah, but we'll make it all clever." She grabbed a blank sheet of notebook paper and started to draw.

"Like this," she said, drawing two stick figures. "I can be a bunch of social media apps. Like a big tablet full of apps." She drew a rectangle around the stick figure, and

then added a little bird icon, and a camera . . . and something else I didn't recognize. "Sorry," she said. "That's supposed to be a thumbs-up. And you—" She drew wings on the other stick figure. "You'd be a butterfly! And together we'd be—"

"A SOCIAL BUTTERFLY! Now I get it!" I could use one of my black ballet leotards and leggings for the body—then all I'd have to do was add wings. Easy!

"So, you like the idea?" Teagan asked. "It's not too silly, is it? Or too complicated?"

"It's just missing one thing," I said, taking the pen from her. I drew a beanie on the first stick figure's head. "*Now* it's perfect!"

Chapter 3

Double Whammy

𝒯he rest of the weekend flew by in a blur. Before I knew it, it was time for my usual Double Whammy Monday evening at Liberty—first poetry, then ballet.

"Come on, Red, just give Liberty Bells a try," I said after I climbed into the car.

"No way," Red said, settling into the front seat beside Mama. "The Liberty Bells sound like a pop band. Not a super smooth, rhymin' and vibin' spoken word group." He turned back to wink at me. "Plus, I've got a rep to protect."

"Sure thing, *Clifford*," I said, using his full name, and rolling my eyes at him for good measure.

"What about the Fresh Princes of Poetry?" Red snapped his fingers. "After that old TV show with Will Smith?"

"If you haven't noticed, three of us are girls." I buckled my seat belt. "Fresh Princesses?"

He gagged. "My rep, don't forget my rep."

Mama laughed. "You two might as well be siblings," she said. "You're just like me and Tonya used to be."

Red had been living with us for six months, ever since his mom—my aunt Tonya—was deployed overseas. He was like a big brother to me now—sometimes an *annoying* big brother. But I loved him, and it was because of him that we had a poetry group.

We shot some more ideas back and forth until Liberty came into view. The building was a majestic fortress of orange-red brick and stained-glass windows, and as usual, a feeling of calm washed over me as we got closer. I knew every inch of that place, from the initials carved into the ancient oak tree out front, the creaking of the floorboards in the center of studio three. Liberty may have been an old building, but for me, it was home.

It meant all the more to me, too, after this summer. The city had threatened to close Liberty after a massive electrical failure was too expensive to repair. If it wasn't for me and the community rallying together to raise awareness and funds, we might have lost our home away from home forever.

Red slid the side door of the car open as soon as we pulled into a parking spot.

"See you later!" we called to Mama.

Time for Change

Isaiah, Teagan, Bria, and Alejandro were already in studio six when Red and I arrived. I slipped onto the floor beside Teagan, eyeing her huge book bag behind her.

"More homework?"

She nodded. "But guess what? I figured out what I did wrong on that quiz, all by myself!" She knocked the side of her head. "Maybe I'll get the hang of this advanced coding stuff after all."

"Of course you will," I said. "I think this deserves an awesome sauce!"

Taking their cue, Bria, Alejandro, Red, and Isaiah joined me in saying "AWESOME SAUCE!" at the top of our lungs, like we always did when someone did something exciting. Teagan beamed.

Red clapped his hands to get our attention. "Okay! We've got five weeks before Voices. Poetry slams are supposed to be more about celebrating the spoken word than who's best. Except there *are* winners. And those winners go to Pittsburgh for the all-state slam . . ." He raised his eyebrows at us as he pulled some flyers from his back pocket. "So let's get down to business. The rules and scoring info are on here. I'll give you a few minutes to read through things."

I scanned the paper. Our slam would be set up like the

high school competition—five rounds, with a three-minute time limit on each poem. No props, no music, no projections or anything fancy like that. It had to be just us poets onstage using our words—*and our bodies*, I added to myself—to perform our poetry. Each team's scores from each round would be added up and the three teams with the highest scores would advance to the state slam.

I skipped down to the scoring criteria.

Judges evaluate two factors of each performance: the writing of the poem itself, and the presentation of the poem. Be creative! Vivid imagery is always a plus. Remember—the best poetry makes people feel something, so make sure you're feeling something up there onstage!

I thought back to all the pieces on Saturday. The poets talked about everything—politics, social causes, love for their families, appreciation of nature—but each poem had touched something in me, making my insides buzz like the ancient sound system at Liberty. That same buzz was building up inside me again.

"So," Red said, once we were done reading, "we need to decide how to tackle each round. I'm thinking we should stick to only two people in each group piece—that gives each poet enough time to share some really meaty stuff within the three-minute limit. That leaves two rounds for

individual poems . . ." He took a deep breath. "Which means not everyone will be able to perform an individual poem."

No one spoke for a few seconds. Some of us would have to give up doing a solo. *Should I volunteer,* I wondered? What if I stuttered too much onstage? Would the judges score lower for that?

"Well, I definitely think *you* should perform," Bria finally said to Red. "You're our best poet."

We all nodded in agreement.

"Aww, you guys are trying to make a brother turn all red over here." He rubbed his neck. "But I don't think that would be fair. Maybe we could draw straws or pick numbers or—"

"I don't mind skipping the solo part," Teagan said.

I turned to her. "What? But, Teagan—"

"Really, it's okay," she said. "I'm already drowning in homework. Taking on two poems might be too much. Plus, I'll have just as much fun doing a duet, as long as I get to do it with *you know who.*" She elbowed me.

"Same with me," Alejandro said. "Basketball tryouts are coming up. I could use a little more time on the courts. Got to work on tightening up my crossover."

Red smirked. "You could have a whole *year* and you still wouldn't have a crossover as smooth as mine."

Double Whammy

Alejandro pulled out his phone. "Want me to show everyone the video of you on the court the other day, when you tripped and—"

"Okay, okay, let's stay on subject," Red said as everyone laughed.

We all fell silent again. I was just about to raise my hand to volunteer to bow out of the solos, but then Isaiah spoke up. "I really think Gabby should give the other poem."

Bria smiled. "I'm so glad you said that! I was thinking the same thing."

What?! I shook my head. "I'll j-just m-m-m-mess up onst-st-stage."

"You're amazing onstage," Bria said. She faced the rest of the group. "Didn't she do great in her ambassadors speech?"

Isaiah nodded. "Gabby, when you talk about things that are really important to you, you're . . . you're awesome sauce!"

"AWESOME SAUCE!" everyone yelled.

"And you and Red give us the best chance to make it to the state slam," Alejandro said.

I couldn't believe they were saying that! I knew I could write a knockout poem . . . but actually saying it onstage

was a whole other thing. Unlike my ambassadors speech, my performance wouldn't just affect me if I messed up. It could hurt the entire team.

"Can I think about it?" I asked. "I d-d-don't want to let you all down."

"Sure thing," Red said. "But don't think too long. We've only got five weeks."

As I nodded, Teagan leaned over and gave me a quick hug. "Don't stress about it," she whispered. "You've got this."

Red picked up his notebook. "Onto the group poems, then. Teagan, you'll work with me."

Her face twisted into a frown. "Oh. Um. Okay." She crossed her arms. "That would be, um, great . . ."

Red held her gaze for a few seconds before bursting into a laugh. "I almost had you! I'm kidding. Teagan, you're with Gabby."

"Yes!" Teagan yelled. Then she composed herself and said, "I believe that would be acceptable."

"Hmm. Imagine that," Red replied, still writing. "Alejandro, why don't you partner with Bria. That leaves me and Isaiah. Everybody feel good about that?"

There was a chorus of "yeps" and "uh-huhs."

Double Whammy

"All right," Red said. "You read the guidelines. We have to feel something up there onstage. Let's take a couple minutes to brainstorm topics for our poems. Everyone individually for now, then we'll break into teams. Two minutes, starting . . . NOW!"

I grabbed my DREAM BIG notebook and turned to the first page. During the ambassadors election, I'd learned just how important passion was when you wanted a crowd's attention. I almost sabotaged my own campaign by choosing a platform I thought would be popular instead of one I cared about. I switched it out at the last minute, though, thank goodness, but if I was going to do a solo poem, I wasn't going to make the same mistake again.

Writing as fast as I could, I jotted down some possible topics:

- Dance

Dance had been my passion since before I could walk, according to Mama.

- Leadership

Time for Change

My ambassador platform was all about building unity between the grades, because everyone deserved to feel welcome at school.

– My cat, Maya

On account of how cute and cuddly she was, obviously!

– Poetry

Poetry was a newer passion of mine, but I couldn't deny that it was right up there with dance and my leadership activities. That buzz I felt inside said it all.

I took a breath and reviewed my list. Would people really want to hear about my cat? *Sorry, Maya.* I crossed her off the list. Leadership, Dance, and Poetry were left. All three were my Big Dreams. How could I choose to write about just one?

"Time's up!" Red said. "Let's break up into our teams for the group poems."

Teagan and I moved toward the back wall and got to work brainstorming. She flipped to a poem called "Forever

Friends" that we'd worked on together last month. It seemed like the perfect poem for us to do together!

"Should we read it out loud and go from there?" I said.

"Yeah. Here goes," Teagan said. "Forever friends, through thicker and thinner,"

"Through blackouts, rallies, and a girl named Aaliyah," I continued.

Hmmm, that part doesn't feel right anymore. I'd have to ask Teagan if we could tweak that.

"Through my bumpy speech," I continued.

"And my non-dancing feet," Teagan said. We alternated the next lines until the end:

"Even though I can't speak a lick of code,"

"And I speak HTML, Java, and Go"

"I have your back, your front, and all your sides—"

"Main Line Tech or Kelly,"

"We'll stay best friends,"

"For real—"

"Bona fide."

I smiled. Teagan and I were going to rock it onstage with this poem!

"Well," Teagan said. "For starters, it's too short. That was only thirty seconds!"

"No problem!" I said. "We can easily write more. Should we each brainstorm for a few minutes and then share what we have?"

"Sounds good!" Teagan said.

All six of us were concentrating so hard on our poems, no one realized the time until Stan, Liberty's longtime head of maintenance, peeked his head in the studio. "Alejandro, your ride's outside."

I glanced at the clock. Shoot! I was going to be late for ballet!

"See you all later!" I said to the group. Then I scooped up my things and dashed out the door for the part of my night that put the "double" in double whammy.

Chapter 4

That's the Pointe

I speed walked to studio four and slipped inside, but instead of warming up at the barre as usual, the other girls were sitting on the floor in front of our teacher, Amelia.

"Gabby, you're just in time," Amelia said, tapping her nose. That had been our special way of saying hello ever since Amelia came to teach at Liberty when I was six years old. "Come join us."

I sat down next to a girl named Natalia, wondering what was up.

"So, my little flowers . . ." Amelia began, a huge smile on her face. Our recital piece last year was the "Waltz of the Flowers," and she'd been calling us "her little flowers" ever since. "I've been really impressed with everyone's progress this year, which is why I have an announcement!"

"We're going en pointe?!" Natalia guessed. "OMG!!!"

Time for Change

Really?! I'd been looking forward to going en pointe ever since Amelia showed us her toe shoes that first year she was here!

"Close," Amelia said, chuckling. "I mean, yes, though not en pointe 'for real' for a while. I'd like to start doing pre-pointe work with you—first on demi-pointe, then in a few weeks, we'll have a field trip to get your first pair of pointe shoes—"

"AWESOME SAUCE!" I yelled, only to have ten pairs of eyes flip toward me.

"Whoops. S-s-sorry," I said, laughing at myself. "Poetry thing. My b-b-bad."

Amelia chuckled again. "You'll get your pointe shoes and we'll start wearing them for some work at the end of class each week. I'll tell you right now—you're not going to step away from the barre for quite a while. This year, we will focus on strengthening your body to support you in pointe shoes, and go back to the basics on alignment. You'll have some homework, too."

A few girls groaned.

"Don't worry," Amelia said. "The homework's not much. Worksheets on ballet vocabulary and things like that. I even have some anatomy coloring pages."

Coloring homework sounded fun! Or give me a whole book to read, I didn't care—I was getting pointe shoes in just a few weeks! Natalia and the other girls looked excited, too. Mandy, who had her long hair tied up in a huge bun on top of her head, was up on her knees, like she might jump up any second and bounce onto pointe, toe shoes or not.

But Amelia's smile disappeared. "Pointe work is serious stuff. You can really hurt yourself if you don't know what you're doing. It's going to be hard work—maybe even boring sometimes. So I need you to think carefully about whether you're ready for this commitment, okay?"

We all nodded, though I didn't need to think about it. While I loved tap, there was something just . . . *magical* about ballet. Maybe it was the stained-glass windows in studio four or the classical music Amelia used for our exercises, but sometimes, I felt like I was in church while in ballet. Class was always comforting and challenging at the same time.

"Excellent! I'm glad you're all so excited!" Amelia said. She rose and motioned for us to do the same. "Let's get to work, shall we?"

She explained that pointe work required strength in not only our ankles and feet, but our legs and torsos, too, so we'd begin with an exercise using our stomach and back muscles today. She had us sit on the floor under the ballet barre, facing the wall.

"Our goal here is to keep our torsos vertical—long and strong!" she said. She put the bottoms of her feet flat against the wall in front of her, and scooted her bottom in until her knees were bent in a demi-plié position. Then she sat up really tall, and with her arms rounded in first position in front of her, she pushed against the wall with her feet. That pushing made her legs straighten, which made her pelvis and whole upper body slide away from the wall. The entire time, she kept her torso straight up and down, as solid as one of the columns in the lobby of the Liberty theater.

"Your turn, ladies!" she said. "Use your abdominal muscles to keep your torsos long and strong!"

I scooted in and put my feet against the wall. Sitting up straight couldn't be that hard, right?

Wrong. If I pushed gently and slid slowly, it was pretty easy to stay long and strong like a column, but if I pushed harder against the wall and slid out faster, my torso wobbled all over the place. I'd have to practice this one!

We went through more exercises, Amelia correcting us along the way. After a few repetitions of an exercise where we stood facing the barre and "rolled up" to relevé on both feet, my ankles and feet felt like Jell-O! Amelia had to remind

me a few times to keep my ankles pressed together in proper alignment, and to keep my torso long and strong.

"Excellent, Gabby!" She finally said, when I'd done three roll-ups correctly. "That's what I love about you! Even when the going gets tough, you never give up." She tapped my nose and moved on to the next student.

I smiled. It was true—I never gave up, even when I wasn't sure I would succeed. This summer, I didn't know if we'd raise enough money to keep Liberty open, but I organized a benefit performance anyway. I never thought I'd win the ambassador election at school, but I pushed through. Giving up wasn't an option when I was Dreaming Big.

Suddenly, I knew my answer for Red. I had to do a solo at Voices, even with my stutter, because not doing one would be like giving up before I ever started.

"Gabby?"

I blinked. Amelia was trying to get my attention. "You okay? We've moved on to another exercise."

I quickly looked at the other kids. They all had one hand on the barre, ready for pliés.

"I'm s-s-s-sorry," I said.

"No problem. But try to stay with us."

I shook my head to refocus my brain on ballet, and sure enough, as my body folded itself into the correct positions,

my mind followed along. By the time we moved to center work, I'd pushed aside all thoughts of poetry.

Well, almost all thoughts.

I still remembered the buzz inside my belly while brainstorming just an hour ago.

The buzz I'd felt when I'd heard the Pink Poetics on Saturday.

The buzz I felt every time I put my thoughts into words on paper and then spoke those words aloud.

I was starting to think that I'd never completely forget about poetry ever again.

DREAM BIG by Gabriela McBride
First draft

When I think of my dreams
I remind myself
a seed doesn't know
what kind of flower it will become
But it pushes up through the soil
no matter what
until it reaches the sun

That's the Pointe

And when I think of my dreams
I remind myself
a butterfly isn't born with wings
It has to build a cocoon first

But what if a seed was scared
of the sunlight above?
Preferred to stay comfy
in its soft, cool soil?

What if a caterpillar
never built a cocoon?
Just stayed a worm
inching along?

The seed would never know
the beauty it could be

The caterpillar would never feel
the joy of flying free

Chapter 5

The Enchilada Court

"Wait up, Gabby!" Aaliyah was rushing through the hallway toward Ms. Tottenham's classroom. She nodded toward the door as she came up beside me. "Excited for our first ambassadors meeting?"

"Sure th-th-thing," I said. Then I looked down at the floor. "And maybe a little nervous." I couldn't wait to make good on my campaign promise of helping the grades get along better, but I had no idea how to start.

"You've got this," she said, pushing the door open for me. "And remember, I've got your back in there."

"And I've got yours," I replied.

Ms. Tottenham smiled as us as we took our seats next to the seventh- and eighth-grade ambassadors. Ms. Tottenham was our social studies teacher, and also the ambassadors' adviser, not to mention the funkiest fashionista around.

The Enchilada Court

Today she was wearing a flowing beige shawl with black pants, a black turtleneck, and a bunch of wooden bracelets.

"I'm glad to see you all so bright-eyed this early in the morning!" Ms. Tottenham said. As she talked, her bracelets knocked together and I relaxed a little. The clacking reminded me of Daddy typing away on his computer while I fell asleep at night.

"Since this is our first meeting," Ms. Tottenham continued, "why don't we introduce ourselves? And to help us get to know one another, how about we each give a fun fact? I'll go first." She cleared her throat. "I'm Ms. Tottenham and I like to make jewelry." She shook her wrist.

Everyone turned to look at me. I guess I was next.

"I'm G-G-Gabby . . ." I paused for a moment. I knew what I wanted to say, but it was like my words were having stage fright—they didn't want to come out. Real quick, I checked in with myself, moving my jaw back and forth. It felt tight, like a stretched rubber band. If I wanted to get the hard-G sound out, I had to relax it, so I took a deep breath and started over again. My speech therapist, Mrs. Baxter, taught me that trick.

"I'm Gabby McBride, and I like poetry." Then I thought for a moment and added, "No. I *love* poetry."

The seventh-grade ambassador squinted at me. "Hey,

you were the girl on the news this summer. You did that dance thing in the park, right?"

I nodded. "Yep. We were raising money for Liberty Arts Center." I laughed. "I guess I should have said that I love poetry *and* dance."

"Well, you're certainly very good at both of them," Ms. Tottenham said. "Thank you, Gabby. Aaliyah, why don't you go next."

Aaliyah laced her hands together and looked out at everyone. "I am Aaliyah Reade-Johnson. I like . . ." She sat up taller in her chair. "I like punctuality."

Ms. Tottenham covered her mouth, stifling a smile. So did the other two ambassadors.

"That's great," Ms. Tottenham said, composing herself. "Thank you, Aaliyah."

The eighth-grade ambassador, Sondra, went next—she liked playing strategy games. And then the seventh-grade ambassador introduced himself. His name was Bryson, and he liked basketball. I wondered if he ever played with Red and Alejandro.

"Fabulous," Ms. Tottenham said. "Now on to ambassador business! I know you're all eager to get to work carrying out your campaign platforms, but as you know, the other

part of your job is to help plan school functions. And our first one is right around the corner."

"You mean the Halloween party?" Bryson asked.

Ms. Tottenham nodded. "I'll be meeting with Principal Reedy this afternoon to discuss it." She motioned toward Sondra and Bryson. "You two were here last year. Do you have any suggestions for this year's party?"

"I do," Sondra said. "There's always plenty of candy. But I bet kids would eat other snacks, too. Maybe popcorn?"

Aaliyah's hand shot up. "I helped my mom prepare food for a Halloween party last year. We had pumpkin truffles, and these apple and marshmallow snacks that looked like fangs. And maybe we could even have red punch like blood? Or maybe . . ." She stopped once she realized everyone was looking at her. "I'm sorry. I really like theme parties, and creative recipes and crafts and stuff. Maybe I should have said *that* for my fun fact."

I smiled. I had learned last week that Aaliyah's mom had a catering business and Aaliyah often helped her, but I didn't know she liked doing crafts. Teagan and I were always making things.

"Hey, I'm all for creepy Halloween food," Bryson said.

"As long as the snacks aren't *too* healthy. It is Halloween, after all." That made us all laugh.

"These are all great ideas," Ms. Tottenham said. "We'll also need to think about decorations for the gym, and flyers to announce the costume contest."

"I could get some of the guys from my homeroom to help with decorations," Bryson said. He looked at Sondra. "And maybe you could get some eighth graders to help with flyers? Didn't the eighth graders do that last year?"

As Ms. Tottenham reviewed how the tasks were split up last year, I couldn't help but notice that the grades hadn't worked together at all. The eighth graders handled one thing and the seventh graders another. It sounded like the sixth graders had hardly participated in the planning or even the party itself. Apparently only a handful of sixth graders entered the costume contest. Were they too afraid they'd be teased by the older students?

Well, I had promised to do something to unify the grades. Maybe now was the time to start.

I raised my hand. "Yes, Gabriela," Mrs. Tottenham said.

"How is the costume c-c-c-contest set up?"

"The teachers and staff serve as judges. There's usually a winner for each class as well as an overall winner," she said. "Why do you ask?"

"Well, I was w-w-wondering if there was a way to get the classes to work t-t-t-together, in the planning, but also at the party itself? To build community, like I talked about in my speech. Maybe the costume contest could be done in teams or something?"

"I think Gabby's on to something," Aaliyah said. "And so the older kids don't leave out the sixth graders, every team has to include at least one sixth grader?"

I nodded and gave Aaliyah a big smile.

"There's no way the seventh and eighth graders would go for that," Bryson said, his voice squeaking as he talked.

"I think it sounds great," Sondra said, straightening her glasses. "Maybe it'll encourage more sixth graders to participate."

Ms. Tottenham clapped her hands. "I say we do it. Great idea, Gabby and Aaliyah!"

Aaliyah sat up at her desk. "And as leaders of the school, we should probably dress up as a group."

"I'm in!" Sondra said.

"Me, too!" I added.

Bryson didn't look so sure. But then he sighed. "I guess this is the kind of thing I signed up for when I agreed to be an ambassador, right?" His face became serious. "But I need

final veto power over our costume. I've got a rep to protect, after all."

I rolled my eyes. What was it with seventh graders and their *rep*?

"Fantastic!" Ms. Tottenham said with a chuckle. "I'll take everything to Principal Reedy this afternoon."

As Bryson started talking about robot costumes, Ms. Tottenham walked over to me and Aaliyah. "Great job, guys," she whispered. "You two are going to make excellent ambassadors."

"Is it edible?" I asked Isaiah as he placed his school lunch tray down on the table. His chicken enchiladas looked like two lumps of dirt drenched in watery cheese. I had already tried the rice—it was soggy and clumpy.

"The vegetables are decent," Isaiah said, popping a green bean into his mouth. "I wonder if they do that on purpose. Make the main dish so horrible that you're forced to eat the vegetables." He opened his milk container. "I was looking for you this morning. Where were you?"

"She was with me." Aaliyah came up behind me, her lunch tray in her hand. Somehow, her food had been laid

out perfectly, just like that perfect bun on top of her head. Maybe the cafeteria workers were afraid to mess up her tray.

Isaiah slid over to make room for Aaliyah as she said, "So, any thoughts about what we should dress up as?"

We quickly explained the new rules for the costume contest to Isaiah. "I should find Red," he said. "He'd be a great partner."

"Oooooh! You should dress up as old English playwrights," I said. "Shakespeare and . . ." I paused. I didn't know any other old English playwrights.

"Or maybe you guys could be poets," Aaliyah said. "Langston Hughes and Edgar Allan Poe. He wrote scary stuff, didn't he?"

"Sure did," Isaiah said, his eyes widening at the sheer sogginess of his rice or the horror of Edgar Allan Poe. I wasn't sure which one.

Aaliyah turned to me. "Think we could get Bryson to dress up as a poet? Would that be okay with his *rep*?"

That made me laugh. "It's going to be impossible to find a costume cool enough for him."

"What if we dress up like old-school movie monsters? You know—like Frankenstein or Dracula? Bryson's so tall, he'd make a super scary werewolf, don't you think?

Time for Change

You—hmm—you could be the Bride of Frankenstein, and Sondra could be a mummy maybe, and then I could be—" She stopped, then shifted in her seat. "Sorry. Like I said, I really like theme parties. I can get a little carried away sometimes, with food *and* costumes."

"No, that's okay," I said. First cooking and crafts, and now costumes. What else was Aaliyah into? "I think it's a great idea. We should run it by the others to see what they think."

"You realize this means you're going to have to make two costumes," Isaiah said to me. Teagan must have told him about our social butterfly plan.

"Wow, two costumes?" Aaliyah said. "We could come up with another idea that's easier—"

"It won't be that big of a deal," I said, shrugging her off. "Plus, I can get really into making stuff, too." I turned to Isaiah. "Remember those bracelets Teagan and I made over the summer?"

Isaiah picked up his last green bean. "Yeah, you're probably right. If anyone can handle all that, you can."

"You bet I can," I said.

We spent the rest of lunch daring one another to eat bigger and bigger bites of soggy enchilada.

"If you're so into cooking," Isaiah said, picking up the

last of his drooping, drippy food and dangling it in front of Aaliyah, "how about you help the cafeteria make these look more appetizing?"

"I've got skills, but I'm not a miracle worker," Aaliyah said. She laughed. "But one day, I'll make you guys my mom's specialty. She's the Queen of Chicken Verde Enchiladas."

"So . . ." I said, grinning. "Does that make you the Princess of Enchiladas?"

"Princess?" Aaliyah crossed her arms and pretended to think hard. "It does have a nice ring to it."

As Isaiah laughed, I stood up from the table and bowed toward Aaliyah. "Your Highness, it has been a pleasure to dine with you this afternoon."

"A pleasure indeed," Aaliyah answered, with a regal nod of her head.

"Well, then," Isaiah said, standing up, too. "We shall dine together on the morrow, my ladies. Until then, I bid you farewell. Adieu!"

Aaliyah and I dissolved into giggles as Isaiah strutted off like a prince—or maybe a jester—in the Enchilada Court.

Chapter 6

Duets

Bzzzz. Bzzzz.

I groaned as I fumbled through the dark, searching for my phone. It took a second, but I finally silenced the alarm.

I couldn't believe I was waking up.

At five o'clock in the morning.

For the third day in a row.

These past two weeks had gone by in a hazy, blinding blur. The preparations for what we were calling the ScareFest were going great, but they were a lot more work than expected. Even with the extra classmates we recruited, there was still so much work to be done. I had hardly started my Bride of Frankenstein costume, or even figured out how I was going to make my butterfly wings, and Halloween was only a week and a half away.

But this morning wasn't about either of those. This

morning was about revising the duet poem, because in just three days, the poetry group was having our very own mock poetry slam. (Red was letting me call it the "Liberty Bells Battle" even though we still hadn't officially decided on a team name.) This afternoon's poetry meeting was our last chance to finish our poems before memorizing them over the weekend, so if I wanted to make changes, I had to make them now. My "Dream Big" poem was in good shape, but the duet wasn't ready for battle. Not yet.

About forty-five minutes and approximately seventy-five yawns later, I had some new lines for the duet. Maya hopped down from my bed just as I closed my notebook.

"Happy Friday, sleepyhead," I said, rubbing her behind her ears.

She purred for a few moments as if to say "I could do this all day," but seemed to change her mind a second later. She jumped over to my furry chair, curled herself up, and went right back to sleep.

If only I could be so lucky.

"Okay, guys!" Red said at the beginning of poetry that afternoon. "I've got some news."

"You fixed your three-point shot?" Alejandro asked.

Time for Change

"No, I—"

"I knew it, man!" Alejandro laughed. "Your three-point shot is hopeless!"

Red just shook his head. "I *meant*, our Voices registration is due tomorrow. We need a team name." Red frowned at me. "And before you start—no Liberty Bells."

"I wasn't going to say that!" I said. "Well . . . I probably wasn't going to say that."

Bria cleared her throat. "I've got some ideas." She pulled her hair into a ponytail, then opened her notebook. "How about: Liberty Bards, Liberty Chime Rhymers, Liberty Beatniks, 'Verse of the Free, Land of the Free Verse, Haiku-nauts—"

"Hold up! Back that bus up one stop," Red said. "Land of the Free Verse. I like the sound of that." He closed his eyes and began nodding to himself. "Land of the Free Verse, home of the poetic. Where masters of consonance and connotation are better than any crew in the entire nation." He opened his eyes and grinned at us. "What do you guys think?"

Teagan raised her hand. "Um, that was kind of long. Can we stick with the short version?"

Red laughed. "Okay, okay. How about just Land of the Free Verse? Thoughts?"

Duets

One by one, we nodded our heads in agreement. I still liked Liberty Bells, but with Land of the Free Verse, I could picture us strutting onto the stage, just like the Pink Poetics had. The name carried confidence in it.

"Perfect!" Red said, clapping his hands. "It's agreed then. I now pronounce us Land of the Free Verse! Let's make some noise by giving Bria an . . ."

"AWESOME SAUCE!"

"All right," Red said. "We've got our mock slam—" He stopped and looked at me. "Before you ask, yes, we can still call it the Liberty Bells Battle."

"Yeah!" I said. "Thanks, cuz!"

"We've got our mock slam on Monday, so let's work hard today. We'll hear Gabby's poem now. Then we'll split into teams to work on the group poems. If we have time at the end, I'll do my poem. Snap your fingers if you're on board with that plan."

"Way to build the slam atmosphere, bro!" Alejandro said.

"Gabby—you're on!"

I jumped up, notebook in hand. Using one of the techniques Mrs. Baxter taught me to help my words come out more smoothly, I closed my eyes for a second and pictured the words of the first stanza of my poem in my head. When I had the words there good and solid, I opened my eyes and began.

Time for Change

"When I th-th-think of my dreams
I remind myself
a sss-seed doesn't know
what kind of fl-fl-flower it will become
But it pushes up through the sss-soil
no matter what,
until it reaches the sun."

I continued, gaining confidence as I went. This next stanza was my favorite.

"What if a caterpillar
never built a cocoon?
Just stayed a www-worm
inching along?"

I finished the poem and nodded my head to show I was done. I'd stuttered a little, but I was proud of how it went.

"Way to lay down some smokin' verses, cuz!" Red said. "See, there's a reason we chose you to do a solo poem! Now, who's got some feedback for Gabby?"

Isaiah raised his hand. "I love how you used the image

of a seed pushing through the earth to say how you never give up. I think a lot of people can relate to that."

"I have something," Bria said. "I liked how you asked a question at the end—it grabbed my attention and made me wonder how I would answer it."

"But also," Teagan piped up, "aren't caterpillars not really worms? I sort of got distracted by that. Maybe try something else there?"

That was a good point. Maybe I could rework that line.

"Okay, great," Red said. "Now let's get to work on those group poems."

I followed Teagan as she bounced over to our usual spot against the wall. Even with her heavy backpack, she looked like she was walking on springs. She couldn't have liked my poem *that* much, could she?

"Look!" Teagan said as we sat down. She held up a loose sheet of paper. "My teacher returned this today!"

It was a test—one with *A* written on the top. "Teagan! This is . . . is . . ." I grinned. "It's awesome sauce! I knew you could do it!"

"I know, right!" We leaned in and hugged each other. "It finally feels like all that studying is paying off. It was

definitely the right decision to pass on the solo for Voices. Plus, this gives me more time for my Halloween costume. Want to work on them on Sunday?"

I shook my head. "Can't. We're getting our pointe shoes! What about Saturday?"

She shook her head. "Grandpa and I have plans to—"

Teagan and I both ducked as a balled-up piece of paper came flying at us. Red sat across the room, staring at us. Then he picked up a pencil and motioned for us to get started writing.

"Okay, okay, we get it," Teagan said as she opened her notebook.

"I wrote some more lines for the duet," I told Teagan. "Want to hear them?"

"Of course!" Teagan said. "I wrote some, too. But you first."

I pulled my notebook closer to me, then began to read.

"Friendship is love
and standing together.
It's silliness,
seriousness,
be-with-you-ness."

Teagan smiled. Be-with-you-ness was one of my favorite things about our friendship, and I knew she loved it, too. How we could sometimes just sit quietly and "be alone together." I continued:

> "It's standing up for a friend who's defenseless.
> It's laughter,
> and jokes,
> like the Enchilada Princess.
>
> A friend is a gift
> like a chest full of treasure.
> The more friends you have,
> the greater the pleasure."

I put my notebook back down. "That's it," I said. "What do you think?"

"I like the first part," Teagan said, squirming a little. "But what was that line about enchiladas?"

"Oh," I said, "it's just this thing from school with Isaiah and Aaliyah. I wanted to put in how friends have inside jokes and stuff—things that are only funny to them, you know?"

Teagan nodded, an odd look on her face. "It's . . . sort of random," she said. "Like, the audience might not get it."

That was another good point. But I really loved that line. It made me smile on the inside *and* the outside when I said it. "But don't you think it's kind of funny, even without knowing the joke?" I asked. "Maybe we can at least try it out at the battle on Monday? See what the reaction is?"

"Yeah, I guess," Teagan said. She shrugged.

I thought she maybe had more to say, but she just sat there quietly for a few seconds. It felt different from our usual be-with-you-ness.

"Want to do your lines?" I finally asked.

Teagan glanced at the clock. "That's okay. Let's just use what we had before, plus your new lines."

"Um, okay," I said, though we still had more than five minutes left. Teagan was being weird. "So, for Monday, how about I say the first stanza, you the second, and me the third?"

"Yeah, that works," she said. Without a word, she copied the lines down in her notebook.

Teagan had been so happy only a few minutes ago when she showed me the test from school. Had I said something to upset her?

"Tell me more about what's going on at Main Line," I said, giving her a little poke on the knee.

She was silent for a moment, but then a big smile spread across her face.

"Actually, there's a fall festival next weekend on Saturday and Sunday! There'll be all sorts of games—egg tosses, tug-of-war, and even a three-legged race!"

We both giggled. Teagan and I had competed in the three-legged race every year at our elementary school carnival. One year, we won these ginormous stuffed octopuses. We'd named them Otto Octopus and Colonel Cephalopod.

"So what do you think?" she asked. "Want to come?"

"It sounds like fun," I said. "Count me in!"

"And did I tell you about this super-cool coding project we're doing?" she continued. "All the sixth graders are creating video games using the coding language Pascal. The first place team wins a brand-new laptop!" She began bouncing a little as she described the project.

"That sounds neat," I said after she finished. "Who else is on your team?"

Her face twisted in confusion. "What? Oh, well, you can have a few people per team, but you don't have to. I like working by myself. More control over the project, you know?"

I thought she might continue, but she just sort of sat there, so I changed the subject and told her more about the ScareFest.

"I don't know how you're doing it all, Gabby," Teagan said, shaking her head. "You've got ambassadors and your individual poem, and our duet and pointe, and your other dance classes, too—"

"I'm fine," I said, my voice a little more forceful than I intended. First Isaiah and Aaliyah, now Teagan. I knew I could do all this.

How come they didn't?

Chapter 7

Pointe Shoes Day

I woke up with a start on Sunday morning to classical music blasting throughout the house.

I *knew* that melody. That was the "Waltz of the Snowflakes" from *The Nutcracker*! What was going on?

Daddy and Red burst into my room, doing their best impression of ballerinas, though they looked more like two ostriches hyped up on caffeine. I busted out laughing.

"Time to get up, my sleepy snowflake," Mama said from my doorway. "It's Pointe Shoes Day!"

My heart did a little happy dance, but at the same time, my eyes flicked to check the clock. I had been getting up super early on weekdays, but I counted on sleeping in on the weekends. It wasn't even nine o'clock yet! Why did Amelia have to schedule this field trip so early?

Daddy and Red curtsied and then headed back

downstairs with Mama. My muscles ached as I climbed down from my loft bed. I'd spent yesterday at school hauling bales of hay into a back corner of the gym in preparation for the ScareFest. It was fun hanging out with Sondra, Bryson, Aaliyah, and the other kids who were helping, but I was sore today. Ms. Tottenham was always telling us that leadership required strength of character, but apparently it required some physical strength, too. Was my body even up for trying on pointe shoes?

Forty-five minutes later, Mama and I met Amelia and the other girls at the dancewear shop.

"Happy Pointe Shoes Day!" Amelia said as we stepped inside, the bell on the door tinkling behind us. She came over and wrapped me in a big hug, then grabbed Mama, too.

"I bet you've been dreaming of this day for quite a while, huh?" Amelia said to Mama when we pulled away.

"You bet," Mama said. "Since . . ." She thought a moment. "Well, since I found out we were having a daughter, honestly."

Wow. I thought *I'd* been dreaming about my pointe shoes for a long time!

"Go ahead and join the other girls, Gabby," Amelia said. "The manager said she'll be with us in a few minutes."

I walked past the racks of leotards and ballet skirts to

the shoe area at the back of the store. Natalia and some other girls were seated on a poofy couch near a wall mirror and the shortest ballet barre I'd ever seen. It was just long enough for maybe two dancers to stand at. The girls were taking pictures of the stacks and stacks of pointe shoe boxes lined up along the wall. Natalia let out a giggle as she and Mandy posed for a photo.

"Gabby!" Natalia's mom said as I walked up. She grabbed Natalia's phone from her. "Why don't you get in there, too? I'll take a pic of all three of you."

As I put my arm around Natalia, I realized this was the first time I'd seen these girls outside of ballet class in at least a year. We used to hang out all the time, but ever since Red started the poetry group, I guess I'd been hanging out with those friends instead.

A few minutes later, Amelia introduced us to a woman named Deborah, who was going to fit us for our shoes. Mama got her phone ready to take photos. All the other moms did, too. I smiled, thinking how it seemed like the moms were more excited than us dancers were, but then I looked to my left. Natalia was bouncing on the couch and Mandy was smiling so big I could see the braces on her back teeth.

I flashed back to my awesome sauce outburst when

Amelia told us we were getting our pointe shoes. Did I feel awesome sauce excitement right now? Not really.

You're just tired, I thought.

Deborah had us take our shoes and socks off, then she examined all of our feet. She called out shoe brands and sizes while an assistant pulled boxes of shoes from the wall. Deborah explained how our toes had to have enough room to properly work inside the shoes—our toes had to be straight, not curled, when we were en pointe—but the shoes also had to be snug enough to support our feet. The pair Deborah picked for me were extra narrow.

"Like mother like daughter," Mama said, slipping her foot out of her own shoe and wiggling her skinny toes. The moms giggled.

Once every girl had a pair of shoes in front of her, Deborah gave us some padding to choose from. There was lamb's wool, gel pads, or if we were really brave, Amelia said, we could cut off the toes of a sock and just use that. I picked the lamb's wool because I could use as little or as much as I wanted.

Deborah showed me how to place the wool around my toes, then gently slid the shoe on my foot. It was so stiff! And heavy!

Pointe Shoes Day

"Go ahead," Deborah said to me once the second shoe was on. "Go try them out at the barre."

I stood up from the couch and immediately wobbled.

"Whoa there," Mama said, coming over to offer me a hand. "They feel a little funny, right?"

I nodded. "They feel b-b-bumpy on the b-b-bottom!"

Mama laughed. "You'll get used to the thick soles."

She walked me to the barre, where I grabbed on with both hands. Slowly, I did an exercise from class. The shoes crackled as I rolled up to demi-pointe, then all the way up to my toes. I was almost as tall as Mama like this!

"Hear that?" Amelia said, coming up behind me. "That sound is the glue in the shank and box breaking down. The shoes will mold to your feet and become more flexible as you dance in them more."

Deborah pinched various parts of the shoe as I did some more exercises, finally nodding to herself. "We hit the jackpot with this first pair in terms of fit! How do they feel?"

"Pretty g-g-good," I said. "I think."

"And how do *you* feel," Mama said to me, holding up her phone. She was taking a video. "My little dancer, all grown up!"

I smiled for the camera and did a couple more roll-ups

to full pointe, but didn't answer Mama. I didn't know exactly what I'd expected to feel when I slipped on these shoes I'd dreamed about forever and ever—maybe something like that buzz I'd felt at the Voices slam. But if I was being honest, today didn't feel that different from any other time we'd come here for new ballet or tap shoes. And speaking of tap shoes . . .

"Mama," I said, nodding toward a shelf to my right with all sorts of fancy taps on it, including a pair that was hot pink and turquoise. "Can I try on some tap shoes while we're here?"

Mama stopped filming, a puzzled look on her face. "I guess so, Gabby, if you're done with the pointe shoes. We have to wait for the other girls to finish up, anyway. We thought we'd all go to Franklin Fountain for root beer floats afterward to celebrate. How does that sound?"

I glanced at Natalia and Mandy. What were we going to talk about at Franklin's, other than ballet? Mama and I were supposed to go shopping for my Bride of Frankenstein costume, too, but I still had to memorize both my solo and the duet before tomorrow's Liberty Bells Battle. And my shoulders were starting to ache from the hay bales again.

"Is it okay if we just go home?" I asked Mama. "I have some things I need to do."

Pointe Shoes Day

"Sure, Gabby," Mama said. "If that's what you want. Let me know when you're ready."

As I took off the pointe shoes and we checked out, Mama made chitchat with the cashier. They traded stories about their own first pairs of pointe shoes.

"Just imagine," the cashier said to me as she handed us our bag. "This'll be you someday, telling your own kid about the day your biggest dream came true."

On the drive home, I tried to picture a scene like the cashier described. But when I imagined telling someone about the day my biggest dream came true, I couldn't get any words out. My stutter wasn't the problem in this imaginary conversation—with my stutter, I knew what I wanted to say and just couldn't say the words. In this case, I didn't even have any words to say in the first place.

It wasn't until later that night, after Mama helped me sew the ribbons and elastic on my shoes and I'd memorized my "Dream Big" poem, that I realized why.

I couldn't picture the day my biggest dream came true, because that day hadn't happened yet.

Voices was still three weeks away.

Chapter 8

Liberty Bells Battle

All right, I said to myself. *Time to try without the notebook.*

I'd been sitting in Mama's Liberty office for half an hour trying to memorize our "Friendship" poem for this afternoon's Liberty Bells Battle.

I took a deep breath, turned my notebook so I couldn't see the words, and gave it a go.

Approximately three minutes later, I'd actually gotten through the whole thing!

Maybe.

I glanced at the notebook to check. Nope—I'd missed one line in my third stanza.

Maybe Mrs. Baxter's "picture the words" technique works for memorizing things, too, I thought. I leaned my elbow on the desk and closed my eyes.

Liberty Bells Battle

The next thing I knew, I was waking up to someone knocking on the door and a sticky note from Mama's desk stuck to my cheek.

"You coming, Gabby?" Stan stood in the doorway, his thumb hooked in a belt loop on his coveralls. "Don't want to be late." Along with Mama and Mr. Harmon, Stan was a judge for the mock slam.

"Thanks," I said, shaking the sleep out of me. "I'll head to the studio in a minute. I want to run through this poem one more time."

Stan shook his head. "Change of plans," he said. "Everybody's in the theater."

I sighed. Red sure was taking this mock slam seriously.

Little did I know *how* seriously.

In the theater, my Land of the Free Verse teammates were seated in the front row, where a RESERVED FOR POETS sign was taped. Mama, Mr. Harmon, and Stan sat in the second row, dry-erase boards on their laps. Red was whispering to them, probably explaining how things would go. A couple of seats away, one of Mama's older dancers was checking her phone, a black stopwatch around her neck.

Red had found a timekeeper, too?! I half expected a DJ and emcee to pop up from backstage at any second.

A nervous flutter started up in my belly, but one smile

from Mama turned it into an excited buzz. I couldn't wait to share "Dream Big" with her. And I wanted to hear everyone else's poems, too, especially Red's. He'd written about Aunt Tonya and had been working really hard—I could often hear him through the walls at night, reciting the poem to himself.

I took a seat beside Teagan.

"Hey," she said. "I wondered where you were. Ready?"

"Yep," I said. *At least for my solo*, I added to myself.

"Great," Teagan said. "And I hope we get some good feedback today. There's only two and a half more weeks to make our poem the best it can be!"

"I'm just going to review the duet one more time before we start," I said, opening up my notebook.

"Okay, poets and judges," Red said from the stage a few minutes later.

I looked up. Someone had turned on the spotlight, making everything seem all the more real.

"Thank you for participating in this year's Liberty Bells Battle," Red continued, "the best mock poetry slam this side of the Delaware River! I'm Red Knight, your emcee *slash* award-winning poet *slash* leader of the phenomenal Land of the Free Verse *slash*—"

"We get the point, Clifford," Mama said with a smile.

"But we don't have all that much time. Maybe we can get on to the scoring?"

"Oh, sure thing, Aunt Tina. Just trying to keep it real." Red had explained the points to us before, but he reviewed them for the judges. Scores could range from 0 to 10.0, though he'd told me the other day that usually no one got lower than a 7—that was an unwritten rule in youth poetry slams. Points would be deducted if we went over time by more than fifteen seconds. He also reiterated that the scores were based half on writing and half on presentation.

Red looked at the five of us in the front row. "I also want us to give each other feedback today. So be thinking how we can make each other's poems leaner and meaner, yeah?" He clapped his hands. "Let's get started! Can I get an 'All right'?"

"All right!!"

"Bria and Alejandro, you're up!"

They climbed up onstage and faced each other, Alejandro's hair long and flowing and Bria's big and bushy and beautiful. I closed my notebook in my lap as Bria began.

"My older brother hates when I wear pink.
He says it's girly, it's weak.

Time for Change

He says I have to be tough.
I'm not one to be messed with,
I'm too smart to be bested.
I love my bro, but I protest it.
'Cause when did the color of my clothes
correlate to my toughness when tested?"

Beside me, Teagan snapped her fingers. I found myself leaning in just like I had at Voices. Alejandro came in next.

"My little brother does nothing but play music all
       day,
earbuds pressed in tight, head bobbing hard.
Can't ever get him in the yard
to shoot hoops or throw a ball.
I just want him to fit in—
that's all.
Be like the other guys.
It's easier if you play—
it's *safer* that way."

They alternated a few more stanzas, then closed out the poem by facing each other and trading off lines, first Alejandro, then Bria, all the way to the end.

Liberty Bells Battle

"But love ain't bound—"

"By colors—"

"Or sports."

"You've got your bro's back—"

"And he's got yours."

I stomped my feet as Bria and Alejandro finished—I couldn't help it! Next to me, Teagan clapped so hard my ears hurt. Isaiah and Red hollered.

Red walked to the front but didn't take the stage. "While our judges gather their scores, let's do feedback. Who has something they liked about the poem?"

"Me!" I said, scooting forward on my chair. "Bria, I liked how you used imperfect rhyme at the end of your verses—it works really well." Red had been teaching us a lot about poetic devices lately.

"And you also did a really good job using alliteration at the end of your first verse, with all the C's and T's," Isaiah added.

Bria smiled. "Thanks. I was hoping someone would notice."

Teagan raised her hand. "I have some constructive feedback."

"Let's hear it," Red said.

"You guys were looking at each other a lot—which I think is okay, but sometimes it was hard to hear you. Maybe try to look out at the audience more."

"Good one," Red said. "Judges, are you ready?"

Mama, Mr. Harmon, and Stan nodded, then revealed their scores on their dry-erase boards.

Two 8.5s and one 8.7.

"All right, all right," Red said. "Not bad, not bad. Can we get an mmm-hmm for Alejandro and Bria?"

"Mmm-hmm!"

I added a few extra finger snaps, just because they'd done so well.

"Gabby and Teagan," Red said. "You're next!"

This was it, the moment of truth. I left my notebook on my seat and climbed up onto the stage with Teagan.

"Anytime you want to start," Red said as my heart began beating a mile a minute.

The first lines of the poem were mine. I glanced at Teagan—she didn't look nervous at all.

Well, here goes. I took a deep breath and on the exhale, I launched into the poem.

"Friendship is love
and st-st-standing together.

It's silliness,
s-s-s-seriousness,
be-with-you-ness."

So far, so good. It was Teagan's turn now.

"It's standing beside a friend who's alone.
It's laughter,
and jokes,
kind words through the phone."

I frowned. Teagan had changed the lines about the Enchilada Princess. I thought we'd decided to keep them on Friday. I gave her a look but continued:

"A-a-a friend is a gift
like a chest full of-of treasure.
The more friends you have,
the great-greater the pleasure."

I breathed a sigh of relief that I'd gotten through that stanza. But as Teagan said her next lines, I kept replaying our conversation from Friday. We *had* decided to keep that part, right? Yes, I was sure of it.

Time for Change

"Gabby," Teagan whispered, "it's your turn."

"Did-did you change anything else?" I whispered back.

"Just that one stanza," she said. "Now you pick up with 'A friend is a raft . . .'"

"A-A-A friend is a raft-raft-raft," I said, the spotlight feeling hot on my skin. "Like a . . . a . . ."

I was drawing a complete blank.

"Through choppy seas," Teagan filled in for me. Then she gave me a look to continue.

But I had nothing. Not one word. Not even if I closed my eyes like Mrs. Baxter taught me.

When I didn't come in, Teagan barreled through the rest of the poem—both her lines and mine. I found my footing again during the last stanza, which we were supposed to say together, but I stuttered so much, I doubted anyone could even understand what we were saying.

After we finished, Red, Bria, Isaiah, and Alejandro clapped. But they didn't holler, or snap their fingers, or stomp their feet.

I didn't blame them.

But there was someone I could blame. She was standing right next to me, her lips pressed together into a thin line.

Red didn't look at me as he walked to the front. "While

our judges gather their scores, any feedback for Gabby and Teagan?"

There were a few moments of silence, and then Bria raised her hand.

"You both had good energy at the start, and came across very passionately about your friendship." I gave her a small nod to thank her for the comment, but I could tell she was just trying to be nice.

Alejandro spoke next. "I can really see the potential in the poem. I think you just need to practice together more."

"Oh, don't worry," Red said. "I foresee a *lot* more practicing in their future." He looked at Mama. "Now let's see what the judges have to say."

But Mama held up her finger to signify that they needed another minute. I took the chance to step closer to Teagan.

"You made changes!" I said.

"Only a line or two," Teagan replied. She shrugged. "Just at that one part."

"But you threw me off!"

"Oh." Teagan looked down at her toes, then quickly back at me. "Sorry I didn't tell you ahead of time. But to be fair, I bet if you'd had the poem better memorized, you probably wouldn't have messed up."

Time for Change

I narrowed my eyes at Teagan. That sounded like something Aaliyah would say, not my best friend.

"We're ready," Mr. Harmon said.

"First, just a reminder that we were told to score half on writing and half on presentation," Mama said. "We liked the writing—a lot—but felt we needed to take off points for presentation."

Mama, Stan, and Mr. Harmon all turned their dry-erase boards around.

6.3, 6.2, and 5.9.

So much for no one getting lower than a 7.

There was silence in the theater as Teagan and I made our way back to our seats.

"Okay, okay . . . that's okay," Red finally said, though he didn't really sound like he meant it. "But let's try to be more prepared next time, poets. From what I've watched of other groups online, we're going to have some steep competition. We can't get to Pittsburgh without everyone giving this their all." He glanced at me as he said that.

I balled my hands into fists so hard, my fingernails left little crescent moon imprints in my skin. Red was accusing me of not giving my all? He knew how often I'd been getting up early and cramming in writing time between things to get my poems done! Just wait until he heard my "Dream

Big" poem. He wouldn't be able to deny that I was prepared for that.

And the duet—I'd done my best. If Teagan hadn't made those changes, I'd have been fine. Probably.

"I'll go next," Red said, hopping up on the stage into the spotlight.

I had been so looking forward to hearing Red's poem, but now I wasn't in the mood. I scrunched down in my chair as Red looked out at the audience.

"This poem is for my mom," he said. Then he shook out his jitters, took a step forward, and started.

"Some see her as a pretty face,
striking in her beauty.
Some see her as a single mom,
always and forever on duty.
Some see her as a doctor,
rocking multiple degrees.
Others see her as a soldier,
stationed overseas."

I didn't want to like Red's poem, but it was hard not to. He really was a good writer. And he was a dynamic, energetic speaker, too, only I kept getting distracted by how

much he was moving around the stage. He was a bundle of nervous energy.

When he was done, everyone clapped, stomped, and snapped, including me. I only gave him baby taps on the floor, though, not full-on stomps.

Teagan raised her hand before people had even stopped clapping.

"Hit me, Teagan!" Red said. "I'm ready!"

"I can tell you worked really hard to memorize your poem."

Ouch. She was talking to Red, but I had a feeling that comment was really more for me. It was like I could hear her adding *just like how I can tell how hard Gabby* didn't *work on ours.*

"Thanks, Teagan," Red said.

Bria, Isaiah, and Alejandro all shared positive comments, too.

"I'm lovin' the love, guys," Red said, "but I know you've got stuff I could improve on. I mean, I may be the Prince of Poetry, but I'm not perfect." He flashed his chipped-tooth grin.

"You can say that again!" Alejandro shouted. Everyone laughed.

Well, everyone but me. I would get up there and show Red how wrong he was about me. But if he thought I wasn't

giving this my all, then I wouldn't. I didn't have to share my feedback about his moving around onstage.

"Okay, then," Red said, actually sounding disappointed that no one had critiques for him. "Let's see what the judges say."

Mama, Mr. Harmon, and Stan turned around their boards.

Two 8.9s and one 9.1.

"Thank you, thank you," Red said, taking a little bow. Then he found Isaiah in the audience. "Isaiah! Why don't you come on up and join me for our group poem."

"Red, just a moment," Mama said. She turned to me. "Gabby, it's time for ballet. You better go."

I glanced at the clock above the theater doors. She was right.

"But I haven't done my solo—"

"That's okay—you can go," Red said, as if he actually preferred that I leave.

"But I really want to do my poem!" I said to Mama. "Can't I stay for just a few more . . ."

I didn't even bother finishing my plea. The look on Mama's face said she'd already made up her mind.

Chapter 9

Unprepared

Had Red purposely left me to go last after the way my duet with Teagan went? I wondered as I made my way to studio four for ballet. It was Teagan's fault I'd messed up, but it seemed like Red was punishing me.

Teagan's comment for Red that was really meant for me stung the most, though. She knew how much I had on my plate. Plus, it was just a mock poetry slam, not the real thing. We'd practice more, and I was sure it would go fine.

Considering how mad I was at Red and Teagan, you'd think I'd want to be anywhere other than the theater, but I found myself walking as slowly as I could to get to ballet.

Did I really have to go tonight?

What about next week?

Or the week after that?

Unprepared

I shook the thought out of my head. I was just feeling rotten about not getting to do my solo poem. I didn't want to quit ballet.

Did I?

No way, I told myself, picking up my pace. Poetry was becoming my Biggest Dream, but pointe was the dream I'd had the longest. I couldn't give up now just as it was about to come true!

At the barre, I threw myself into our warm-up. By the time we got to our tendu combination, most of my anger about the mock poetry slam had drifted away. There was that ballet magic.

Ballet Magic, I thought to myself, *that would be a great title for a poem.*

"We're going to try something different for tendus today, ladies," Amelia said, snapping me out of my thoughts. "Let's see if you can follow along."

I was used to Amelia not demonstrating for the tendu combination. Instead, she liked to test us on our ballet vocabulary by giving us instructions verbally. I secretly loved the challenge of knowing all the French terms.

But when Amelia started talking, it was like she was speaking an entirely different language. She used words

like "adduction" and "abduction." I heard her say something that sounded like "dorsal fin," too. Those weren't French . . . were they?

A few of the other girls looked just as confused as I did, including Natalia, but a couple seemed confident. When Amelia started the music, they began the combination like usual. I followed along, tenduing my leg out to the side, then pointing and flexing my foot, but I was at least a beat behind.

Amelia stopped the music halfway through the exercise . . . or what I could only guess was halfway through.

"Well," she said, raising her eyebrows. "I can see who did their homework . . ."

I slapped my forehead. I'd forgotten all about my pointe homework!

"Dancers, as you've probably already noticed," Amelia continued, "pointe work requires a much more precise knowledge of which muscles you're using and when. Those anatomy worksheets are key. Not knowing that 'dorsiflexion' is another way of saying 'flex your foot' isn't that big of a deal now, but when we get into more technical exercises, you're going to need to know those types of terms. We're going to move on now, but let's make sure those

Unprepared

worksheets are done for next week, okay?" She looked right at me on that last part.

Amelia didn't seem all that mad, but I couldn't help feeling like I'd disappointed her. This Double Whammy Monday was turning out to be a double dud.

We moved on to center work, but all traces of the ballet magic were gone. I couldn't focus on anything. How badly did I want to go en pointe if I couldn't even remember to do my homework?

"All right, girls," Amelia finally said, a big smile on her face, "it's the moment you've all been waiting for. Go get your pointe shoes and bring them to the barre. We'll do our demi-pointe exercises first, and then put on our shoes."

There was more than one squeal as everyone rushed to their bags. I checked in with myself. Still no awesome-sauce excitement.

It didn't come when Amelia had us race one another to see who could tie their ribbons the fastest

It didn't come when the whole class posed for a photo in front of the DANCE! sign Mr. Harmon painted years ago.

And it didn't come when Amelia said, "I'm so proud of you girls, my beautiful dancing flowers! Now come grab a worksheet for next week. And remember, if you put your shoes on at home, wear them *only* at a barre—or a dresser or

countertop—and do *only* the exercises we do in class. You promise?"

We all nodded.

I was in slow motion as I gathered my things. It had been a *long* day.

"Everything okay, Gabby?" Amelia asked, coming up behind me with next week's worksheet.

"Um, yeah," I said, taking the printout. "I-I-I'm ssss-sorry I didn't do the homework."

Amelia put her finger under my chin and lifted it up until we were eye to eye.

"I appreciate that, Gabby. And I know you've got a lot going on. The homework is really important, though. I can't give you as many corrections if you come unprepared and spend all your time just trying to keep up. Do you want to dance en pointe?"

"Yes," I said. *I think*, a little voice inside me added, before I could stop it.

"I'm glad," she said, giving me a hug. "I know it's something you've wanted for a long time. But it takes two of us to get you there." She pulled away but left her hands on my shoulders. "I'm only half the team, right?"

I nodded. "I'll remember the homework for next week. Thanks, Amelia."

Unprepared

"You're welcome."

I expected her to tap her nose like always, but she just reached for the light switches and turned them off one by one.

Standing there in the studio, I couldn't help but think that my love for ballet was being flipped off, too, one class—or maybe one poem—at a time.

No More Ballet?

If I do not go en pointe
would there be a point to that?
What if my heart's not in it
when other people's are?
And what if—
What if—
Can I even think it?
What if I did no ballet at all?
Could I?
Would I?

Could I really give up my
ballet shoes and the barre?
Pliés and chassés?

Time for Change

Tendus and fondus?
What would happen to my feet
if they could no longer leap
along the Liberty floor?
Would I be me anymore?

Later that evening, I curled up on the couch and texted Teagan. Something Amelia said had stuck with me.

I'm sorry I wasn't prepared today. I know that our poem being such a mess meant we missed an opportunity for good feedback. We're a team, you and me. I'll try to be a better teammate next time.

A few minutes later, Teagan texted back.

It's okay. And I'm sorry I was so mean. I wasn't being fair. We both have a lot going on.

I breathed a sigh of relief that she wasn't angrier with me. I typed another message.

Thanks for understanding. Can you send me your new lines so I can get familiar with them?

Sure thing! Are you okay with the changes?

My fingers hovered over the phone. *Was I?* Teagan

Unprepared

was probably right—maybe the Enchilada Princess line was distracting.

Yes, I'm okay with them. A second later, I added: *So we're okay?*

Yep, Teagan responded. *We're best friends. We're always going to be okay. And you can make it up to me by helping me win the three-legged race at the carnival on Sunday!*

I typed in a bunch of fall-themed emojis, then two octopuses. *Deal!*

A few minutes later, I knocked on Red's door on the way up to my room.

"What?" he said, opening the door, then started to close it again when he saw it was me.

"I-I, I just wanted to say—"

"Be quick," Red said. "I'm talking to my mom."

"Oh, okay," I said. "Just . . . I'm ssss-sorry for not-not being more pr-pr-prepared today."

Red sighed. "I know you've been working hard on your solo, Gabby," he said. "But every poem counts the same. Just remember that, okay?"

"Yeah," I said. "Thanks. Say hi to Aunt Tonya for me." Red nodded and closed the door.

"Maya," I said, when I got to my room and found her

waiting for me. "You don't know how to add more hours to a day, do you? That's what I need."

She just swished her tail as if to say "I'm a cat, silly, not a wizard."

"All right, then," I said. "It's going to be another early wake-up call tomorrow. You've been warned."

Chapter 10

Friends

"Did you get the pic I sent?" Aaliyah asked in the hallway before school on Thursday.

"Yes!" I said. "Your mummy costume is going to be amazing!"

"Thanks! The gauze is soaking in tea at home today so it will look all old. How's your costume going?"

"Ugh," I said. "I think I found a wig worthy of the Bride of Frankenstein, but I need to put a white streak in it. And I don't have a dress to wear yet. My mom and I had to cancel our shopping trip last weekend because I had too much other stuff to do."

"Hmm . . ." Aaliyah looked me up and down. "I might have something you could wear." She snapped her fingers. "Hey, what if I came by Sunday to help you finish?"

Aaliyah at my house? That would be weird. Teagan was

pretty much the only friend I ever had over. But I did need the help.

"You know, that would be really great," I said. Then I snapped *my* fingers. "But Teagan and I are supposed to go to the carnival at her school. You can't come Saturday instead?"

Aaliyah sighed. "I promised that I'd help my mom on Saturday. She's got a big event to prep for."

I wasn't sure, but it looked like Aaliyah's shoulders were sagging. I thought she was just being nice . . . but maybe she really wanted to hang out this weekend. "You know what? Teagan said the carnival was all weekend. I bet we can go on Saturday instead. You should come over on Sunday."

"Really? Do you want to double-check with Teagan first?"

I shook my head. I knew it wasn't a sure thing that Teagan could go to the carnival on Saturday, but the more I thought about it, the more I realized it didn't matter. My Bride of Frankenstein costume had to come first. Along with pointe and poetry, leadership was one of my Big Dreams. And I had a duty as ambassador to really put my all into the ScareFest.

"Come over on Sunday," I said to Aaliyah. "I'll text you my address."

Friends

That night, once I finished my homework, I grabbed my laptop to video chat with Teagan. Maya purred loudly in my furry chair, as if to rival the video chat ringtone.

"Hey!" I said when Teagan appeared onscreen. She was sitting at her kitchen table—I recognized the faux-wood wallpaper behind her. "Are you doing homework?"

"Yeah, but I can talk for a second," she said. "I'm working on my Pascal coding project." She began bouncing in her chair as she described her progress. I only understood every fifth word, but I was glad to see she was still happy about school.

"That sounds so great," I said after she finished. "So . . . about the carnival this weekend. What if we go Saturday instead of Sunday? And then we could work on our social butterfly costumes afterward?"

She looked back at me, worry across her face. "You can't go Sunday?"

I shook my head. "I thought I could, but it's the only day I can work on my costume."

She frowned. "Your butterfly costume? But you said—"

I looked down at my lap. "No. M-M-My costume for the Kelly Halloween contest."

"Oh." She pulled a pencil from behind her ear and began twirling it. "Well, I can't go on Saturday. The robotics club is taking a field trip to Temple University to view the computer labs."

"That sounds like fun."

She just shrugged. "Yeah. Maybe. But if you've seen one computer lab, you've kind of seen them all."

Who was this girl I was talking to on the screen?! Certainly not Teagan. She lived for anything that had to do with electronics and computers. "I guess I have to skip the carnival, then. I really wish I could go, but you know how it is. The ambassadors are counting on me."

"Yeah, I understand." She put her pencil behind her ear again. "I should get back to work. I'll see you tomorrow, okay?"

"Yeah," I said. "See you at poetry."

She waved good-bye, then disappeared. After shutting my laptop, I went to pick up Maya, only to realize she'd slipped out of the room. I needed to hug *something*—I felt like I was a dart in one of those balloon carnival games and had just popped Teagan's excitement. So I walked over to my closet and pulled out Otto Octopus.

You would think that with eight arms, Otto Octopus would have been a good hugger, but he was nowhere near as cuddly as a cat.

Friends

I got a text from Teagan Sunday afternoon, right as I was finishing my lunch.

Hey. I made some changes to our poem. I was thinking that instead of these lines:
A friend is a gift
like a chest full of treasure.
The more friends you have,
the greater the pleasure.

We could use these:
Some friendship is a treasure,
all the riches you'd desire.
But true friends work best
when only two are required.

I had to be honest: While I understood her reason for taking out the Enchilada Princess part, I didn't see how this change was going to improve our poem.

More than that, I didn't agree with what her new lines said. True friendships weren't just limited to two people. Sure, Teagan was my *best* friend, but I had other true friends. Isaiah and Red. *And Aaliyah, too,* I thought.

Can I take a closer look and we'll talk tomorrow? I texted back.

Okay.

Time for Change

Great! Have fun at the carnival! I pressed SEND and headed upstairs—Aaliyah would be here soon and I still needed to clean my room. I had just made my bed when another text came in. It was from Amelia, with a photo attached.

Look what popped up online on my page—this was four years ago today! You've grown as a dancer so much since then! Can't wait to see how much you'll grow in the next four years! Xoxo!

The photo was from right after Amelia came to teach at Liberty. Teagan and I had been "helping" her clean up after one of her classes. In the photo, I was sitting on the floor with Amelia's pointe shoes on my feet—they were much too big, of course—with the ribbons pooled around my ankles. Teagan crouched behind me, her arm wrapped around my shoulder. We both had several teeth missing from our gigantic smiles.

I put some clothes in the hamper. *Four years from now. Would I even still own pointe shoes?* Ever since I'd written that poem about no more ballet earlier this week, I'd been pretending I was going to quit, just to see what that felt like. When Sondra and Aaliyah made Monday night plans to prepare food for the ScareFest, I thought how I could have helped, too, if I didn't have ballet. Before I grabbed my dance bag for tap on Wednesday, I took out my ballet shoes and pointe shoes. My bag felt lighter, but so did I. And yesterday,

Friends

while I completed my ballet homework, I thought how I could have been writing poetry instead.

A line from Monday's poem came back to me as I wiped some dust off the dancer figurine on my dresser: *Would I still be me without ballet in my life?*

I wasn't totally sure, but I was leaning toward *yes*.

There was just one thing still worrying me. Well, two *someones* worrying me: Mama and Amelia. Every time I imagined telling them I wanted to quit ballet, I could hardly keep from crying. They'd worked just as hard as I had to get me to this point. Like Amelia said, we were a team. Could I let them down like that?

I couldn't figure out how to respond to Amelia's text, so eventually I just sent a heart emoji. The doorbell rang a second later.

Of course Aaliyah would be right on time.

I took a deep breath to clear my head, then headed down the hallway. Aaliyah met me halfway up the stairs, a few strands of hair poking out of her usually perfect bun. She wore an old pair of jeans and a thick, oversized sweatshirt. It was the first time I'd ever seen her look so normal.

"Your mom said I could come on up. I brought every-thing I could find that I thought might work for your costume." She held two plastic bags with fabric spilling out of each.

"Thanks," I said as we entered my room.

"Cool! You have a loft bed!" Aaliyah said. "I've always wanted one of those!"

I nodded at Aaliyah, wondering what her bedroom looked like. An image popped into my head: a tidy space, perfectly clean with pencils and craft supplies arranged in neat bins along some shelves.

She dropped her bags on the floor. "And who's this?" She went over to my bed and picked up Otto.

"Oh, just something I won at a carnival once," I said, grabbing him back. For some reason, I didn't want Aaliyah touching him.

"Cute!" Aaliyah said, then she kneeled down in front of the bags. "First things first—let's see how this dress looks on you." She pulled out a long, flowy white dress with sheer arms and boxy shoulders. It looked really similar to the one in the *Bride of Frankenstein* movie!

"That's perfect!" I said. "But it's really long!" I could have climbed on Aaliyah's shoulders and the dress would have covered us both.

Aaliyah pulled out a box of safety pins. "Don't worry! We can fix that, no problem. Want to put it on?"

Friends

She stepped out of the room as I changed. When I glanced in the mirror, I couldn't help but laugh. The sleeves went way past my fingertips, making it look like I had skinny, floppy wings.

"You can come back in," I yelled through my laughter.

She opened the door, then giggled. "Yep, too long and waaaaay too big." She took a pin out of the box. "Just keep still."

"Are you sure this is okay?" I asked. "I don't want to mess up your dress."

"It's my stepsister's, not mine," she said. "And it's no problem at all. My sister's already outgrown it, and I don't see myself wearing it."

"You have a stepsister?" I shook my head. "Every time we talk, it seems like I learn something new about you."

"Same here," she said. "Like I didn't know you had a cat until I got here. Your mom said she's named Maya. Like the poet?"

I nodded. "Yep. I got the idea to name her after Maya Angelou after we read—"

"'Life Doesn't Frighten Me,'" Aaliyah said. "In class last year." She smiled at me. "Don't forget, I was there, too."

I laughed. Aaliyah *had* been in my class . . . but we hadn't been anywhere close to being true friends. Or even good friends. Or even people who liked standing next to each other, if I was being honest.

"So how are your poems going?" she asked.

Teagan's request popped into my head.

"They're fine, I guess. But both still need work, and the competition is only two weeks away."

"Isaiah was telling me all about the slam," she said. She took a long time with the next pin. "I was thinking about coming. Would that be okay? I wouldn't want to make you nervous."

I'd been so glad to see Aaliyah in the crowd during my ambassadors speech. She'd made me feel anything *but* nervous. "I would love for you to come," I said. "And Isaiah would, too, I bet." Aaliyah smiled big.

"We could practice your poems after I finish the dress," Aaliyah said, moving to work on the sleeves. "Would it be helpful for me to say Teagan's part for the duet?"

"I . . . um . . ." I shook my head. "Th-Th-Thanks for offering, but I d-d-don't think—"

"Oh, it's okay," she said quickly, her fingers fumbling with another pin. "I was just trying to help."

Honestly, it probably would have been nice for her to recite Teagan's part. But just like it felt weird for her to touch Otto, Aaliyah saying Teagan's words seemed wrong.

Friends

After we fixed the dress, we got to work dyeing a streak of white in my black wig, then spraying the hair so it stood up just like in the movie. This costume was starting to come together! And that was good—Halloween was only two days away!

As Aaliyah went to put some supplies in her bag, she noticed the black leotard and leggings I'd pulled out a week ago, hoping to get started on my butterfly costume.

"Are those your ballet clothes?" she asked. "Oh! Are you using them for your butterfly costume? They're perfect! But where are the wings?"

"I haven't made them yet." I sighed. "At least, I really *wanted* to make them, but now I'm thinking I'll just buy some tomorrow night. There's just no time . . ."

"Good luck trying to find some the night before Halloween," she said. "The Halloween store probably looks like a tornado blew through."

I hadn't thought about that.

"But you know what?" Aaliyah said. "My mom made some wings for my little cousin last Halloween. You probably already have the stuff you need—just wire hangers and some old tights or panty hose."

"That sounds perfect," I said.

"I can look up instructions right now."

I was so happy to have the wings figured out, I could have hugged Aaliyah. But I didn't. Were we hugging friends yet? I wasn't sure.

"What is it?" she asked. "You had a funny look on your face all of a sudden."

"Oh, nothing," I said. "Just . . . thank you for all your help."

She shrugged. "No problem. That's what friends are for, right?"

DREAM BIG—new lines

A social butterfly
turning into a busy bee
I spread my wings
and spread myself thin
across all my favorite things

The tiny tap dancers in my stomach
push the butterflies to my throat

Friends

and I'm afraid
all the seeds in me
won't bloom

They need so much water!
And care!
And light!
I do what I can
I make sacrifices when necessary

But also:
I'm not the only gardener

When I think of my dreams
I remind myself
that it's okay to need some help
pushing my way up
until I reach the sun
building my cocoon
until I can fly free

Chapter 11

Keep Doing What You're Doing

I shivered in the chilly October breeze. Next to me, Teagan pulled her beanie down lower. Red told us to meet here for poetry today, by the big heart mural the community painted on Liberty's brick wall this summer. Bria, Alejandro, and Isaiah were nearby, kicking around acorns under the ancient oak tree that stood at the corner of the building.

"So . . ." I said to Teagan. "Did you win any giant sea creatures yesterday to keep Colonel Cephalopod company?"

I was expecting Teagan to at least giggle at that, but all she did was shake her head.

"But the carnival was fun?" I asked.

Keep Doing What You're Doing

"It was okay," she said. "It would have been a lot more fun if you were there."

"I know. I would have loved to meet your friends at school. Next time, okay?" I squeezed her hand.

"Yeah," Teagan said. She squeezed my hand back, but for a split second, I felt that weirdness in our usual be-with-you-ness. Maybe I was still just feeling uncomfortable about those lines she wanted me to change. Since we didn't have much more time before Voices, I decided to just go along with them, but I still didn't like what they said.

Or maybe I was just cold. Where the heck was Red?

As if on cue, Red burst out of Liberty's front doors. "Land of the Free Verse! Let's get the power flowin'!"

"Dude," Alejandro said, coming over to the mural. "What's up with the al fresco rehearsal? It's not exactly summer anymore."

Red nodded as we all gathered around him. "Noted, bro. But with only a few more meetings before the big day, we should get serious about prepping however we can. We gotta get used to performing in all sorts of settings, you know? If you can perform out here, with the cold and the cars driving by, and the squirrels squabbling over acorns, you're golden for any stage, right?"

Time for Change

"I guess, man," Alejandro said, "but you owe me a hot chocolate or something."

"Deal," Red said. "And let's go all out for performances and feedback today. No holding back, all right?"

We all nodded.

"Okay. The sidewalk is our stage and the mural is our backdrop. Gabby—you're up!" Red pointed to me. "Everyone else, take a seat in the audience, aka on the bumper of Aunt Tina's car."

I grabbed my notebook and hopped in front of the mural. I couldn't wait to share the new lines I'd added last night! I thought my "Dream Big" poem was just about ready for the slam.

Goose bumps prickled my arms as everyone got settled. I glanced at my notebook one more time, then took a deep breath and began.

"When I think of my dreams
I remind myself
a seed doesn't know
what kind of flower it will become . . ."

That buzz started up in my belly again. I made it through my whole poem only looking at my notebook once. I hadn't

meant to internalize the poem, but somehow, the words were already inside me. I hardly stuttered, either—just once when a car pulled into the lot. By the time I was done, the buzz in my belly had spread to my fingers and toes.

I stood there as five sets of eyes stared at me. There wasn't one snap, not one clap. Even the squirrels were quiet.

"Gabby," Red said, after several seconds of silence. "That was . . ." He couldn't seem to find the words.

"Awesome sauce?" Isaiah offered in a voice so quiet I could hardly hear him.

"No," Red said. "Better. Gabby—you were made for this. Like, it's a part of you, huh? Almost as natural as breathing."

I let out a breath I didn't know I was holding.

Yes. That's exactly how it felt. Like poetry was as much a part of me as the mural was a part of this wall. Like it had roots as big as the oak's reaching deep inside me.

"Any feedback for Gabby?" Red said.

"Just . . ." Bria started. "Just keep doing what you're doing."

"Yeah," Isaiah said. "Whatever you're doing, keep doing it."

"I will," I said, and took a seat on Mama's car.

I planned to do *this* for forever.

Time for Change

"I put mine on on Tuesday, Wednesday, Thursday . . ." Mandy counted days on her fingers as I entered studio four a little later. "Not Friday . . . yes Saturday . . . not Sunday—but only because my mom said I had to let the counter be a counter and not a ballet barre at least two days a week."

"Whoa," Natalia said. She turned to me. "How many times did you put on your shoes since last week?"

"Um . . ." The only time I'd touched my pointe shoes was to take them out of my bag before tap, and put them back in for today. "Zero?"

"Really?" Mandy said, her eyes wide. "I don't know how you did it."

I just shrugged. Between ScareFest prep for tomorrow and working on my "Dream Big" poem, there hadn't been time to even think about putting on my pointe shoes this week. But at least I'd done my homework! Until I knew for sure if I was quitting ballet, I didn't want to disappoint Amelia.

I slipped on my ballet shoes and headed to the barre to begin class. With my body still buzzing from poetry, it was like every cell in my body was fired up and ready to go.

Keep Doing What You're Doing

There was an energy in my movement that I hadn't felt in a long time, like the buzz from poetry was a motor pushing me along. When we moved into pointe work, my torso was longer and stronger than ever. My ankles were solid, my alignment almost perfect. I was pretty sure I had blisters on my feet, but I pushed through, feeling invincible. This wasn't ballet magic, but it was *something*. For a split second, I wondered if I shouldn't give up ballet after all. What if I was missing out by not seeing how far I could go en pointe?

"Great job, Gabby!" Amelia said as she walked around. "You're looking fabulous today. Keep doing what you're doing!"

Her words made me freeze in place. Hadn't Bria and Isaiah said the same thing about my poetry less than an hour ago?

"I will," I responded, and in the moment I meant it. But just as quickly, that little voice inside me added, *but not for long. I'm not going to do* this *forever.*

"Ouch!" I stuck my finger in my mouth. I was trying to make my wings for tomorrow, but as if the blisters on my toes weren't enough pain for one night, I kept poking my fingers with the sharp ends of the wire hangers. That little voice had followed me home and wouldn't quiet down, no matter how many times I shushed it. Some part of me had already decided to quit ballet, it seemed.

Ouch! A wire poked me in the belly. *That's it!* I said to myself. *I have to figure out this ballet thing once and for all.* My wings would have to wait until after school tomorrow.

I put my pajamas on, grabbed my journal, and climbed into bed, my blisters stinging as they hit the sheets. I flipped to a new page in my notebook.

Reasons to NOT quit ballet and pointe:
I'm so close to going en pointe for real!
Mama and Amelia would be disappointed
It would be neat to see how far I could go en pointe

Reasons TO quit ballet and pointe:
More time to work on my poetry
More time for leadership activities
I don't really have any friends in ballet anymore
No more blisters!
No more ballet magic anyway?

Keep Doing What You're Doing

I was most unsure about that last one. Did I really not like ballet as much as I used to, or was I just so tired lately that I wasn't enjoying it as much?

I reviewed my lists as Maya hopped up onto my bed. There were more reasons to quit than to stay, but the reasons to stay somehow seemed more important.

"What am I going to do, Maya?"

She answered by rubbing her face against my ear and letting out a meow that sounded almost like "Ma."

"You're probably right," I said. "I should talk to Mama about this. Maybe after tomorrow, with tomorrow being Halloween and all. Sound good?"

Maya curled up in a ball and closed her eyes, so I did the same.

No More Ballet—revision

Could I really give up my
ballet shoes and the barre?
Pliés and chassés?
Tendus and fondus?

Time for Change

What would happen to my feet
if they could no longer leap
along the Liberty floor?

What would fill my heart
if I gave up this dance?

But even as I question it
I know what the answer would be
I know what would fill ballet's space
It's on this page
staring back at me

Chapter 12

Trick or Treat

R ise and shine!" Mama woke me up early the next morning so we could get me decked out as the Bride of
Frankenstein.

She helped me put on the dress, then we wrapped my
arms in strips of gray fabric just like in the movie. As I
climbed up on her bed so she could put the wig on me, she
noticed my blistered feet.

"Goodness, Gabby," she said. "We should get you some
tape for your toes before next week's class. And then later I
can show you how to soak your feet in Epsom salts."

"Um . . . okay," I said. Maybe now would be a good
time to talk to Mama about ballet after all. I gathered my
courage as she put the wig on my head and made sure it was
extra poofy.

"This looks great!" Mama said after she'd emptied

approximately half the bottle of hairspray on the wig. "Time for makeup. Scoot closer to me and I'll do your eyeliner."

We got really close, face to face, Mama being careful to not bump my blisters as she did so. I looked right into her green eyes as she drew thick liner on my lids. I was about to tell her how I was feeling about ballet when I noticed something else.

"Mama?" I said. "Are you crying?"

She laughed. "You caught me. It's just . . . your first blisters from pointe shoes—I'm so proud of you, Gabby. A lot of dancers don't get this far in their training. I've been bragging to my friends all month that my little girl's going en pointe."

She grabbed some powder for my face and neck as a prickly ball formed in my tummy. I tried to imagine Mama having to tell her friends her little girl went en pointe . . . and then quit.

"And—we're done!" Mama said. "Take a look!"

Happy for the change of subject, I jumped down from the bed and went over to Mama's mirror.

Whoa! I looked just like the character in the movie!

"Mama! This is awesome-sauce-amazing! Just wait until the other ambassadors see me! Thank you!" I gave

her a big hug. She squeezed me back in the best Mama-hug ever.

"Poet and ballerina last night, Bride of Frankenstein and leader today," she said when we pulled away. "You never cease to amaze me, Gabriela McBride."

I smiled, but would Mama still think I was amazing if I quit ballet? And in that moment I knew I couldn't quit. Wouldn't quit. I'd stick with ballet and pointe. For Mama.

At school, I met Sondra, Aaliyah, Bryson, and some of the art students in the library to help with finishing touches for the ScareFest. Aaliyah, of course, was the best mummy I'd ever seen, with her entire body wrapped in strips of cloth. The tea had definitely made them look ancient and creepy! And Bryson made a great werewolf... except with his gloves on, he couldn't even hold a pencil!

Over the course of an hour, we transformed the hall-ways of Kelly Middle School from boring brick and carpet into a creepy, ghoulish graveyard. Moss hung from the walls, cardboard tombstones lined the hallways, and a huge full moon hung from the ceiling outside the main office. But as cool as the decorations were, what was even more awesome was that it was a mix of all grades doing the work together.

"The eighth-grade hallway looks even better," I told Red when I met him in the seventh-grade hallway before the first bell. Red had on a thin black tie, a tweed jacket, and a fedora—and had even penciled in a thin mustache over his lip with some of Mama's makeup. He was supposed to be Langston Hughes. He knew that most people wouldn't get his costume, but he didn't care.

Neither did Isaiah.

I did a double take as he approached us. Isaiah had on an old-timey black suit with a small black bow tie. A pair of wire-rimmed glasses frames sat on the bridge of his nose, and he had shaved a thin straight line right down the middle of his Afro.

"Way to go all out with the hair," Red said. "I don't know if I could have done it. It's bad enough covering up my fauxhawk with his hat. It kind of itches."

Isaiah laughed. "I figured it would grow back. How many other opportunities would I have to dress up as Dunbar?"

He meant Paul Laurence Dunbar, a famous African-American poet and novelist from the late 1800s.

"I like your costume, too," Isaiah said to me. "You really went all out!"

Trick or Treat

"You should compliment Aaliyah, not me," I admitted. "I wouldn't have finished it without her help."

Ms. Tottenham came over to Aaliyah and me at the end of social studies that day. The ScareFest had gone better than any of us expected. "Look at what you've done after being ambassadors for only a few weeks," she said, beaming. "Principal Reedy is so pleased that he wants to meet next week to see what we can come up with for November."

A November event? But we had just finished the October one! Aaliyah and I glanced at each other. This ambassador role was turning out to be more work than I thought.

The bell rang, though, and I had another problem on my hands.

Only a couple hours until trick-or-treating, and my butterfly costume was still without wings!

"All right," I said to no one in particular when I got home. "I've got ninety minutes to transform from bride to butterfly. I can do this!"

Half an hour later, I'd washed off all my makeup and tossed my dress, the strips of fabric, and wig in the corner of my room. I had on my black leotard and leggings. All I needed now were wings.

I managed to wrangle the wire hangers into the proper shape. The next step was stretching an old pair of tights over the top, which was only one hundred times harder than shaping the hangers. Every time I slipped the tights over the hangers, they ripped. At this rate, I *was* going to have to quit ballet . . . simply because I'd run out of tights.

Forget the hangers. It was time to improvise.

I spun a slow circle in my room. *Wings. Wings. Wings.* There had to be something around here—

Suddenly, Maya shot out from behind one of my curtains. I must have jumped four feet.

"Maya! Oh! Curtains!"

With only ten minutes until people arrived, I climbed up on my loft bed and took down one of my bright pink curtains. It was a little dusty, but it would do.

I fastened the curtain to the back of my leotard with a safety pin . . . or tried to.

"Too bad you don't have hands," I said to Maya, who was staring at me like I'd sprouted wings. Which I guess I had. "I could really use a little assistance with this sheet."

I finally got it attached to the leotard. Then I found some hair ties and put one around each wrist, tucking the corners of the curtain inside.

I stepped in front of the mirror.

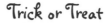

I looked kind of like a butterfly. Maybe.

My hair was a frizzy mess from being under the wig all day. I didn't have time to fix it, though, so I grabbed my Bride of Frankenstein wig and stuck it back on my head. Now I just looked like . . . well, I had no idea.

Red knocked on my open door two seconds later. "Almost ready, cuz? I talked to Alejandro. He and Bria are on their way over now." He frowned as he looked at me. "Um . . . what are you supposed to be again?"

"A butterfly," I said, laughing. "Isn't it obvious?"

"More like a butterfly that flew into one too many windshields," he said, smiling back. "But don't butterflies have antennae?"

I snapped my fingers. "I knew I forgot something." I dug through my stage makeup. "I'll be down in a sec, okay?"

Red ran down the stairs as the doorbell chimed. As fast as I could, I drew antennae on my temples . . . and they looked like nothing at all. So I tried to incorporate the lines into a butterfly shape around my eyes.

Nope, I thought as I stopped to take in my work. The lines did *not* look like a butterfly. They were more of a badly drawn superhero mask.

"Superhero Butterfly Monster," I said. "At least it's original."

Time for Change

I took one last look in the mirror, then grabbed my candy basket and bolted down the stairs. Everyone was already outside.

"Ta-da!" I said, jumping out onto the porch. I put on a cheesy smile to show everyone I knew how ridiculous I looked.

No one said anything for a few moments. Teagan had a really weird look on her face, but then again, I would, too, if I were looking at me.

"Wow," Alejandro finally said, a throwback Allen Iverson basketball jersey loose around his skinny frame and a basketball tucked underneath his arm. "That's, um, really . . . what are you again?"

I held up my arms. "A butterfly. Or a superhero. Captain Monarch?" I offered, giggling.

He laughed. "It's a good thing your poetry skills are better than your costume skills."

"But did you see Teagan's costume?" Bria asked. She had on a pink jacket, like in the movie *Grease*. She pulled Teagan toward me.

Whoa.

Teagan was a giant tablet. Dressed in all gray, she had a shiny black "screen" hanging down her front, like how the

workers at the empanada take-out place across from Liberty sometimes wore signs to attract people into the shop.

"And look what happens when you touch it," Bria said. She pressed Teagan's screen-body a few times. I felt my mouth drop open as hearts, little birds, and thumbs-up emojis appeared.

"That's really cool, Teagan!" I said.

Teagan just shrugged.

"Okay, guys," Daddy said. "Let's get to trick-or-treating. It's a school night, after all."

We waved good-bye to Mama and Mr. Harmon, who were staying behind to hand out candy. Then, as the others began to follow Daddy down the sidewalk, I fell into step beside Teagan.

I cautiously pressed her tummy, and another heart appeared. "Teagan, this is one of the best costumes I've ever seen. How does it work?!"

Teagan didn't answer me for several seconds. "It's an optical illusion," she finally said. "The screen is dark Mylar film, which hides the emojis underneath. But when you press the screen, a sensor relay causes a random part of my costume to light up so you can see what's underneath. One of my teachers lent me some materials and helped me with

it." She moved her candy basket from one hand to another. "It took a really long time, but it was totally worth it, don't you think?"

"Yeah," I said. "Totally. You look A-plus amazing." I gestured to my own costume. "Mine-Mine d-d-didn't quite turn out . . . well, it didn't t-t-turn out like yours. Maybe we should st-st-stick to zombies next year." I put my arms out in front of me and did my best zombie impression, my face all twisted and my eyes crossed.

"Maybe," Teagan said, her voice flat. "Come on. We don't want to get behind."

I fell into step beside her as we walked to my neighbors' house. Mr. and Mrs. Marshall sat outside on their small porch, a large bowl of candy on the ground in front of them. They were dressed up as farmers. Mr. Marshall even had a pitchfork and glasses, like in the famous painting.

"Our favorite Halloween duo!" Mr. Marshall said when we reached their door.

"Our costumes go with each other!" I said. "Want to guess what we are?"

"Hmm," he said, his hand on his chin. "Teagan is a tablet, and you, Gabby . . ." He paused. "Are you guys a super tablet?" He turned to Mrs. Marshall. "Is that some kind of new gadget I haven't heard of?"

Trick or Treat

"You-You got Teagan right . . . sort of." I said. "I'm a b-b-butterfly. Together, we're a social butterfly! Get it?"

He laughed. "Oh, well, of course!" Mrs. Marshall said. "Take some candy. And happy Halloween!"

Teagan grabbed her candy and brushed by me before I'd even put my candy in my bag. She was *really* eager to get to all the houses this year.

"Teagan," I said. "Slow down a little, okay. It's hard for me to walk so fast with my wings."

Teagan didn't say anything for a moment. Finally, she said, "Sorry—it's uncomfortable for me to walk slowly in my costume." She turned to catch up with the others.

Um . . . okay. That didn't even make sense. I was starting to think Teagan didn't want to be trick-or-treating.

Across the street, our group was talking to another group of kids while Daddy checked his phone a few feet away. I recognized Bryson and Sondra immediately. They were still wearing their costumes from school.

"Hey, Gabby," Sondra said once I'd joined them. "What are you dressed up as now?"

"A butterfly," I said, shrugging. "Or maybe a superhero."

"Okay," Sondra said. "That's, um, interesting."

"Well, it's not as rocking as your school costume was," one of Sondra's friends said, just as Daddy stepped to join

the circle. "You guys should have totally won first place in the contest." Teagan had been standing on the outskirts of the group, but now stepped forward, too.

"Whoa, is that a tablet?" Bryson asked. "That's a great costume." He nudged one of the other boys. "Look, it even lights up."

Daddy turned to Sondra's friend. "I heard all about the contest at school, but didn't get to see Gabby in costume. I would have loved to, after she spent so much time working on it."

"It w-w-wasn't *that* much time," I began, looking at Teagan.

"Hold on, I've got a picture right here," Sondra chimed in, pulling out her phone. "Dressing up in groups was all Gabby and Aaliyah's idea." She held her phone up to Daddy.

Teagan slowly inched over so she could see, too.

"Wow, Gabby," Daddy said. "Looks like all that time you and Aaliyah spent on Sunday was worth it, huh?"

Teagan's head snapped up, her mouth slightly open.

Sondra noticed the look on her face as well. "I know, speechless, right?" She flipped through a few more images, then pocketed her phone.

"Let's go!" Alejandro said. "My candy bag isn't going to fill itself!" He took off down the sidewalk with Red, Isaiah,

and Bria close behind. Sondra and Bryson took off in the other direction as I waved. I linked my arm in Teagan's and started forward to follow Alejandro, too, but Teagan's feet stayed glued to the pavement. I turned around.

"That's why you couldn't come to the carnival on Sunday?" Teagan said. "You were working on your *other* costume . . . with *Aaliyah*?"

Whoa. Teagan had tears in her eyes.

"I-I . . . yeah, I was." I reached out and put a hand on her shoulder. Nothing made me sadder than watching my best friend cry. "You know how hard I worked to become an ambassador. Our first event had to be awesome, including our costumes."

"I know how important the ambassadors are to you." She shook my hand away. "But that was before I knew you spent all your time working on that costume instead of ours." She crossed her arms. "Is that why you didn't have our duet memorized at the mock slam? Were you too busy working with Ms. Perfect?"

Now I crossed my arms. "Teagan, don't c-c-c-call her that. It isn't n-n-nice."

"Oh, sorry. I hadn't realized you two had become such good *friends*. If you like her so much, why don't you have her perform in Voices with you, too?"

Time for Change

"Teagan. You're o-o-overreacting," I said. "Who cares what we're wearing for Halloween?" I held up my candy bucket. "The c-c-c-candy tastes the same no m-m-m-matter what we wear."

"Maybe you don't care. But I do. At least, I did."

She pulled out her phone, then pressed a few buttons. "Grandpa? Are you still at Gabby's? I'm ready to go home." She marched toward my house.

I started to run after her, but stopped. She was being ridiculous.

It was a stupid costume.

It's not like we'd be tested on it, or even have to be an example to a whole school in it.

As Teagan disappeared around the corner, I spun around and caught up with the group. None of my neighbors knew I was a butterfly, but I didn't care. The candy still tasted the same.

Chapter 13

Cooling Off

By Friday at lunchtime, I still hadn't heard from Teagan. I slipped into my chair in the cafeteria and considered pulling out my phone to send her a text. Then I decided against it. I hadn't done anything wrong. She was the one getting all worked up about a silly costume. We weren't allowed to have our phones out; I wasn't going to risk getting in trouble just for her.

Besides, there was something else on my mind. Even though I'd told myself I would stick with ballet for Mama, that little voice in my head wouldn't quiet down. The more I thought about it, the more I wanted to quit. I'd have more time for poetry and ambassadors. I had to find a way to tell Mama and Amelia somehow.

I had another problem, though.

Ever since I admitted to myself I wanted to quit, I

couldn't get through the "no matter what" verse of my "Dream Big" poem without stuttering like crazy. How was I supposed to get up onstage and talk about never giving up on your dreams when I wanted to give up on one of mine? I was hoping some more rehearsal was all I needed.

"One more week until Voices," Aaliyah said when she joined me and saw my poetry notebook on the table. "Ready for your big solo?"

"Sort of," I said. "But I'm struggling with a few lines. Do you mind listening to me practice?"

"Of course. No problem."

Isaiah arrived as I opened up my notebook. I handed it to Aaliyah.

"Okay, here goes," I said.

But just like at home, I kept getting tripped up on the lines about pushing on, no matter what. I tried a few of Mrs. Baxter's techniques, like relaxing my jaw and picturing the words in my head, but they only helped a little. Those lines just wouldn't come out.

Aaliyah handed the notebook back to me once I'd finished. "Most of it was good, except for that no-matter-what part. Even when you got your words out, it didn't sound like your heart was in them. Maybe you should change those lines?"

Cooling Off

I focused on my notebook. If I changed those lines, I'd have to change the rest of the poem, and we had only eight days until the slam. "You know, in poetry group, we usually start with p-p-positive comments first."

"I did," she replied, lacing her fingers together. "I said most of it was good, remember?"

"You did seem a little flat overall," Isaiah added. "Is it because of Teagan?"

I quickly shook my head. I'd filled Aaliyah in about what happened, but I didn't feel like talking about Teagan right now, or about quitting ballet. Or about anything, really.

"Have you heard from Teagan yet?" Isaiah asked, not getting the hint.

"No," I said, and left it at that.

"I can't believe you haven't talked to her since Tuesday," he continued. "Have you guys ever gone that long without talking?"

I shook my head and scooped up a spoonful of soggy creamed corn. The longest we'd gone without talking or texting was that summer after I confronted Teagan for always jumping in when I stuttered. But it only took one day for us to make up then. Not two days and counting. No matter what, though, I'd have to talk to her at poetry this afternoon. I forced myself to swallow a bite of corn. Somehow, I wasn't all that hungry today.

"Maybe Teagan just needs a little time to cool down," Aaliyah said. "Remember last year, when Riley Mulligan made fun of her beanie? She didn't talk to him for the entire year."

I quickly put my spoon down, causing a few bits of corn to scatter across the table. "That's t-t-t-t-totally different," I said. "Riley deserved it. I didn't do anything wrong."

"I agree," Aaliyah said. "All I was suggesting was that Teagan seems like the type of kid to hold a grudge for a while."

"But she d-d-d-d-doesn't have any reason to be m-m-mad at me!"

Isaiah quickly looked around. "Gabby, you're yelling."

I took a deep breath, trying to calm down. "Look, Aaliyah, I kn-know you mean well, but you don't understand. R-R-Real friends don't go that long without talking."

"But we go two or three days without talking." Aaliyah shrugged. "Almost every weekend, really."

"Well, yeah. But we're not—"

I froze as her eyes widened. It was like I'd just tossed a cup of ice-cold water in her face.

I immediately knew the words had come out wrong. I

hadn't meant it like that. Aaliyah and I were friends—that I was now sure of. But we weren't *best* friends. She wasn't Teagan.

"Aaliyah," I began quickly, "I d-d-d-didn't mean it like that. It's just . . . it's different f-f-from Teagan and me. It's—"

Aaliyah held up her hand, silencing me. Then, after patting her bun, she stood up from the table. "I guess I'll go eat somewhere else. Maybe with my *real* friends."

I half rose from my seat. "Aaliyah . . ."

She didn't look back as she walked off, her head held high.

Chapter 14

Missing in Action

I decided to get to poetry group extra early that afternoon, so I'd have time to talk with Teagan beforehand. Maybe she'd apologize for the way she'd acted on Tuesday. Or at least tell me what the big deal was about a silly costume.

Red arrived in studio six first, then Bria. With two minutes before poetry group, everyone was there and waiting. Everyone except Teagan.

Red was checking the time, too. His gaze bounced from the wall clock to the door.

Finally, Red clapped his hands. "It looks like we're short a team member. No sweat. Let's break up into groups, and we'll try to track Teagan down." He looked at me. "Can you text Teagan to see where she is?"

"I—um—m-m-maybe you'd better text her."

Red gave me an odd look but shot off a text. It only took

her a few seconds to reply. Frowning, Red walked over and dropped to the floor beside me. "She's swamped with home-work," he said. "But she said that you'd already talked to someone about taking her place in Voices." He put down his phone. "Gabby, what's going on?"

Teagan did have a lot of homework, but skipping practice wasn't like Teagan. It wasn't fair to the team. It wasn't fair to *me*. Was she really *that* mad at me? And what was she even talking about with someone taking her place?

"No one's t-t-t-taking her place," I said. "But we haven't talked since Tuesday."

"Well, you need to figure out how to squash this," he said. "The competition is in eight days."

I just nodded. He stood there a second, like he was choosing his next words carefully.

"You're messing with our Top Three chances right now, Gabby. I'm tempted to pull your duet altogether and have Bria and Isaiah do a duet or something—"

"Why are you m-m-mad at me?" I asked. "Teagan's the one sk-skipping. Not me."

"Oh, don't worry," he said. His face was red. "I'm about to tell her the same thing." He pointed at me. "You two need to fix this. If not, I will."

"I-I know." I nodded so hard my ponytail whacked my forehead.

Red finally relaxed and his face went back to normal. "Go ahead and work on whatever you want." He sighed. "Maybe she'll change her mind and show up."

As I walked over to the wall where Teagan and I usually sat, I couldn't help but think that as mad as Red was, he'd be even more upset if he knew my "Dream Big" poem was now a dud. I was putting the entire team at risk.

Of course, if anyone could help me figure out what to do about ballet and my "Dream Big" poem, it was probably Teagan. Talking to my BFF always made me feel better.

Too bad my BFF wasn't talking to me.

I began revising my solo, trying to find something to replace that tricky part, but I kept getting sidetracked. How could I even think about my Big Dreams when it felt like everyone who was important to me was mad? First Teagan, then Aaliyah. And now even Red. Big Dreams were about tomorrow. I could barely focus on today.

But I knew one thing—I wasn't going to let my team down at Voices like I'd let Teagan down at our Liberty Bells Battle.

I would make this right, one way or another, and I knew exactly where to start.

Chapter 15

Truth

Tiny, invisible tap dancers were tap-tap-tapping in my stomach as I stood outside Mr. Harmon's studio at Liberty the next morning. He was placing easels in a circle. All around him, watercolors, papier-mâché, and collage art lined the wall—you name it, Mr. Harmon had made it.

I could just see the top of Teagan's head through the high window—she always came to help out with her grandpa's Saturday classes. She was sitting on the floor, her beanie bouncing as she nodded at whatever she was doing.

I jumped and let out a yelp as a closet door swung open behind me. A second later, Stan appeared, carrying a push broom. "Sorry to startle you, Gabby. You okay?"

I swallowed the lump in my throat and nodded.

He glanced at his watch, then looked back toward the studio. "Mr. Harmon's class starts in a few minutes. You

might want to go ahead in there." Then he winked. "Sometimes you just have to rip the bandage off."

"Thanks, Stan." I was sure he knew Teagan and I were fighting. Stan seemed to know everything that happened at Liberty.

Taking a deep breath, I knocked on the studio door, then pushed it open. Teagan looked up. She narrowed her gaze at me, then turned her attention back to the color wheel she was painting. It was for Mr. Harmon's lesson, I was guessing.

Mr. Harmon smiled at me. "Ah, Gabby. So nice to see you this morning." He gave off a fake yawn. "I'm going to grab a quick cup of coffee."

Teagan jumped to her feet. "I'll get it for you."

"That's okay," Mr. Harmon said. "You need to finish that before class starts."

Teagan crossed her arms.

Mr. Harmon just smiled and tugged on Teagan's beanie. "Be back in a few."

He walked out, leaving Teagan and me alone. She picked up the cardboard and moved to a table in the corner— as far away in the room as she could get from me.

I inched forward. "Teagan, y-y-y-you can't avoid me forever."

"Shouldn't you be practicing your duet with your new best friend?" she asked, still staring at the poster.

"Teagan . . ." I sat down at the table. Slowly, I pulled the color wheel away from her. "Will you p-p-please explain what's going on? W-W-W-Why are you s-s-s-so mad?"

The silence that followed felt like whatever the opposite of be-with-you-ness was. Like we were miles apart instead of only a few feet.

She finally looked up at me. Her eyes were red, and full of tears. "Why did you leave our costume to the last minute like that? Your other costume was so good."

I took another deep breath. "Teagan, you know how important the ambassadors program is to me. That was our first official event. I had to participate. I had to give it my best."

"But our friendship is important to *me*," she stressed. "Don't you want to give me your best, too?"

"Of course," I said. "But Halloween . . . it's just a silly holiday. There will be another one n-n-n-next year. We can make even better costumes. I won't be so b-b-busy then."

She sniffed and wiped her nose. "Are you sure? Or maybe you'll decide to dress up with Aaliyah instead."

"Th-That's not fair," I said, sitting back in my chair. "I'm allowed to make new friends."

Teagan didn't say anything to that.

"Teagan, I know my costume wasn't as good as yours . . . but it was about being together, not about making the best costumes."

"But do you know how horrible it feels to spend all weekend working on a costume so you won't let down your best friend in the whole world, just to find out she's spent the past month making another costume—an even better costume—with someone else?"

"But I tr-tried to schedule time to w-w-work with you," I said. "You were busy, too."

"Yes, with homework and school projects. But you have all that plus dance classes and ambassadors—and it *all* came before our Halloween costume."

I just sat there for a second, because what Teagan had said was true. I *had* put everything else before our social butterfly costume. But there was nothing wrong with me doing all those things I love, and I didn't feel guilty for spending time with Aaliyah. She was my friend.

Besides, it wasn't true that schoolwork was the only thing taking up Teagan's time before Halloween.

"Well, you weren't j-j-just working on homework all the time," I said, crossing my arms. "You had robotics stuff, and the c-c-carnival!"

Truth

Teagan's face twisted. "If you were really my best friend, you would have realized how much I *hated* that carnival."

I thought back to our conversation outside Liberty. Had that weirdness I felt not been about our poem after all? Had some kid made fun of her at the carnival or something? "But it ssss-sounded fun. You said there was a three-legged race and everything."

Somehow, that made Teagan's face twist up even more.

I stood there awkwardly for a second. Clearly I was missing something—I just didn't know what. Was she mad at me for cancelling on the carnival, even though she said she wasn't? "Teagan, I know it would have been more fun if I was there, and I really wish I could have come with you. It would have been so nice to meet your new friends from Main Line."

"Well, don't worry," Teagan said, taking a deep breath and looking up at me. "You didn't miss anything."

"What do you m-m-mean—" I started.

Teagan stood up. "Not everyone makes friends as easily as you, Gabby. Have you ever thought about that?"

I opened my mouth to respond, but no words came out.

"I'm going to the bathroom," Teagan said, walking

toward the door. "Grandpa's class will be starting soon, so you should probably go."

"Teagan, I . . ." So many thoughts were swirling inside my head. "Can't we talk—"

"Forget about me, Gabby," she said, walking away. "It shouldn't be too hard. You're halfway there already."

Chapter 16

Letting Go

ello?" My voice echoed off the walls of the auditorium. The Liberty theater had four hundred and eighty seats, but I was the only soul in there today. I made my way to the far side of the theater, then scrunched down in a seat and let the big fat tears run out.

Not everyone makes friends as easily as you.

Teagan was working on that Pascal coding project alone.

She'd brushed me off when I suggested that boy from her class come over to play on the drum kit.

And she asked me to change that part of our poem where I said, *the more friends you have, the greater the pleasure.*

I didn't miss meeting her Main Line friends at the carnival because she hadn't made any.

And I had gone on and on about what I was doing with

Time for Change

Aaliyah, even going so far as to include an inside joke about her in our friendship poem. No wonder she'd changed the Enchilada Princess lines.

Worst of all, I'd literally put my costume with Aaliyah ahead of my costume with her.

I pressed my palms to my eyes. When I looked at it that way, no wonder Teagan was so upset.

But . . . how was I supposed to know she was having trouble making friends if she never told me? We were BFFs, sure, but I couldn't read her mind.

How had everything gotten so messed up?

Suddenly, my seat was really uncomfortable. The dancer in me needed to move around to work these feelings out. I got up and walked to the side aisle of the theater where intricately carved wooden decorations covered the walls. Swirls and curlicues, flowers and vines, and some angels, too. Teagan and I used to tell our secrets to the angels, and one time, we traced our fingers in all the grooves we could reach in the entire theater. It had taken all day.

I ran my finger along one of the vines, then looped around a giant flower petal. My finger followed the grooves to a smaller bud, sort of squished between two larger flowers. The carving here was so detailed, but the grooves were

dusty—I'd have to tell Stan these decorations needed some care. Without even thinking about it, I recited some lines from my poem:

"They need so much water!
And care!
And light!
I do what I can,
I make sacrifices when necessary."

I stopped. I'd written that last line after I decided to work on my ambassadors costume with Aaliyah instead of going to the carnival. It had seemed insignificant at the time, but now I saw why Teagan was so upset.

I had been so focused on watering my Big Dreams, I had forgotten about the little ones, like time spent with my best friend. Those little flowers deserved just as much care as the big ones.

I wiped the last of the tears from my eyes.

I wasn't a wizard; I couldn't make more hours in a day.

But I could take away a big flower to leave more water for the little ones. If I'd had my notebook with me, I would have added one more reason to my list to quit ballet:

Time for Change

Spend more time with my friends

I went over to one of the angels and whispered into its ear the decision I hadn't been brave enough to make until I'd almost lost my BFF.

Now all I had to do was tell Mama and Amelia . . . and figure out what to do about my Voices poem.

First things first.

"Mama?" I knocked on her bedroom door, then pushed it open. She was sitting in bed, already in her nightgown, even though we'd just finished dinner. She had a paperback in her hands.

"Hey, Mama," I said. "Do you have a minute?"

"Always, for you," she said. She closed her book and slipped off her glasses as I climbed into bed beside her. "What's on your mind?"

Just come out and say it, Gabby. You can do it.

"I-I-I . . ." A huge lump in my throat cut me off. Mama put her arm around me and I cuddled up next to her. "I-I . . . I want to quit ballet. Pl-Please don't be-be mad at me!"

"Honey!" Mama hugged me even tighter. "I'm not mad at all. A little surprised, maybe, but not mad!"

Letting Go

I let out a giant breath I didn't know I was holding. "Really?"

"Really," she said. "But why don't you tell me a little more about your decision?"

I filled her in on how I wanted more time for my poetry. And more time for my friends. And how I just didn't want to go en pointe as much as I wanted to be a poet and a leader in my school community.

"Gabby," she said, "I'm proud of you. I'm glad you've found something that makes you so happy. And I know how much Teagan and your friends mean to you. It's very mature to make sure you're putting who you love and what you love ahead of other things."

"But, but, you've been so excited about me going en pointe. I'm so close. I'd be giving up on all that. You're not mad at me for quitting, for giving up?"

"Of course not, Gabby," Mama said. She sat up, then pulled away so I could see her face. "When I was your age . . . guess what I wanted to be when I grew up?"

"Um . . . an interior designer?" Mama was a little obsessed with the home improvement shows.

"Nope," Mama said with a chuckle. "A Radio City Rockette. And after college I came to New York to make that happen. I auditioned a couple of times without getting cast, but I worked really hard in classes and eventually, I made it . . . sort of. They cast me in the Christmas Spectacular as a dancing teddy bear."

I giggled, trying to picture Mama in a giant teddy bear costume.

"After the Christmas season," she continued, "the producers said I should audition again next year to be a Rockette—they liked what they'd seen."

"So did you?"

"I did," Mama replied. "And they cast me."

"What?!" I said. My own mother had been a Radio City Rockette, a dancer in the greatest show in the history of dance shows?! This was HUGE. I sat up in bed. "How come you never told me that?!"

"Because I turned them down."

"Why would you do that?!" I was yelling now.

Mama laughed. "Because the previous summer, I had done some dance workshops at the senior center here in Philly and saw what an impact they had on the community. And on me. And as much as I loved being onstage, helping the community felt one hundred times better. So I auditioned for the Rockettes but also started looking for a venue to open my own arts center." She shifted to put her arm

around me again. "I got a call about the Rockettes, and two days later, I found out Liberty Theater was mine to use if I wanted it. And I did want it—more than anything I'd ever wanted before. More than I'd ever wanted to be a Rockette."

"So you just gave up on being a Rockette?" I asked. "After all those years? Right when you were so close?"

"I turned them down, yes," Mama said. "But I didn't give up."

"But you just said—"

"Gabby, sometimes, as we change, our dreams change, too, and there's nothing wrong with that."

I pulled out my DREAM BIG notebook before going to bed. My Voices poem would need a proper revision later, but for now, I turned to the latest draft and wrote one final stanza.

> Maybe dreaming big
> means fewer seeds
> And maybe growing those seeds
> requires not just water
> and care
> and light

Time for Change

but courage, too
Maybe dreaming big
means letting one seed go
in order to give another
the room it needs to grow

Chapter 17

To Infinity

M ama put the car into park, then looked at me. "Ready?"

I nodded, smiling the best that I could. Last night, I had texted Teagan, asking her if I could come over to her house to talk. I kind of expected her to ignore me, or to tell me to stay far, far away, but she had just replied: Okay.

Mr. Harmon had already opened the door before I could even press the buzzer. "It's good to see you, Gabby. You can go on back. She's waiting for you."

If Liberty was my second home, the Harmons' house surely was my third. I ran my fingers along the old, dated wallpaper that Mr. Harmon loved so much, stopping as I reached Teagan's door. I softly knocked.

"Come in," she said.

I pushed the door open and entered the room. Teagan

sat on her bed, her legs curled underneath her. Teagan's room was smaller than mine, but that just made it feel cozier. I'd spent many nights here, making crafts on her baby-blue carpet.

I looked around, not sure where I was supposed to sit. Usually, I would drop onto the bed beside her, but that didn't seem quite right today. "Thanks for letting me come over," I finally said.

She shrugged. Then, as she curled a few strands of hair around her finger, she said, "Thanks for coming. I know it was hard, especially after what I said the other day."

She was right. It had been hard. But I wanted our usual be-with-you-ness back. By having me over, I hoped she did, too.

I cleared my throat. "So, I was th-th-thinking—"

"I shouldn't have said—"

Then we stopped, looked at each other, and blurted out, "I'm sorry!"

We smiled, then laughed, and it suddenly felt easier to breathe in the room.

"Let me go first," I said. "I'm s-s-s-sorry about . . ." I stopped. *Speak on the breath out*, I reminded myself. "I sh-sh-shouldn't have put off our costume until the last minute. I bet it felt like I was putting everything else before our

fr-friendship . . . and-and-and . . . I sort of . . . sort of was. All that other stuff's important to me, but so is our friendship."

"Thanks for saying that," Teagan said, nodding her head.

There was still one thing I didn't understand, though. I took a step forward. "But . . . but why didn't you t-t-tell me you were having trouble making friends at school?"

She shrugged. "I'm not used to having to tell you things. We used to just always be together all the time and so you *knew* things. And . . ." She unfolded her legs and swung them over the side of the bed. "No one wants to admit that they're not making friends. And then you started being friends with Aaliyah . . ."

I slowly sat down on the edge of the bed. "I really do like Aaliyah," I said after a moment. "She's a good friend. But she's not my b-b-b-best friend. You are."

Teagan nodded. "But it wasn't just that you were friends with her," Teagan said. "You were doing things together. She went over to your house. And you never seemed to be able to make time for me." She took a deep breath. "I was a little jealous. Okay, a lot jealous."

I smiled. I knew that wasn't easy for her to say. "The only reason Aaliyah came over was because she was helping me with my costume," I said. "But I'm g-g-going to be one hundred percent honest. I really like hanging out with her. She's really smart, and creative, and thoughtful—" Teagan was looking at me like I'd grown a second head.

"I mean, I-I know it didn't seem like it in elementary school, and she was definitely mean to us last year, but one of the reasons she has so much to say is because she's constantly thinking about things, making observations and coming up with new ideas. Kind of like someone else I know." I raised my eyebrows at Teagan and she gave me a small smile. "And now that I know her, I realize that when she says something that seems annoying or mean, a lot of times, she's just trying to help, in her own way."

Teagan nodded. "There's a few people like that at Main Line, too," she said. "They're not mean, they just say what they want to say, even if it's hard to hear."

I slid a little closer to her. "Teagan, do you really not have any friends at school? What about that boy who wrote that drum program?"

Teagan pulled at a string on her comforter. "He's . . . he's nice, I guess. And really smart. He asked about the poetry I have in my notebook one time. But . . ." She pulled on the string so hard it snapped. "I don't know. He lives on the other side of town in this giant house and his family goes on vacations to crazy places like Antarctica, and—"

"And it sounds like he's really interesting," I said.

"He is," Teagan replied. "It's just . . . he's so different from me, and I never know how to start a conversation. And mostly . . ." She looked up at me. "Mostly, it's just so much harder than being friends with you."

I laughed. "Well, obviously. You've known him for a couple months and me for a bajillion years!"

"I know," Teagan said, smiling a bit. "But I don't even know what to talk to him about, besides school and coding stuff."

I knew that feeling. Like how Aaliyah and I only talked about school or ambassadors before we started eating lunch together. A smile spread across my face as I remembered the Enchilada Princess day.

"Maybe try bonding over the disgustingness of school lunch?" I suggested with a laugh.

"Except the lunches at Main Line are actually *good*," Teagan said.

"Oh, right."

"I see what you're saying, though." Teagan took a deep breath. "And if you can be friends with Aaliyah, I can make some friends at Main Line, I know I can. It's just . . . now you and me feel different, too." She blew a strand of hair hanging in front of her face. "Things are never going to be like they used to be, are they?"

I shook my head. I'd realized that, too. "Remember when we had different teachers in third grade, though? It was hard and a little weird at first, but we still stayed best friends. And we won some really cool octopuses. Or is it octopi?" I raised an eyebrow and smiled at her.

Teagan sat up. "Both are correct! Although, you could also use 'octopod,'—" She paused, then sighed. "Let's just go with octopuses."

As I laughed, she said, "See! This is why I can't make new friends."

I laughed. "That's not true! You just have to find the people that like you for you, like how I found Aaliyah. Seriously, though." I grabbed her hand. "I want you to make friends at Main Line, and me at Kelly, b-b-but you'll always be my best friend."

"I know," Teagan said. "And you're mine. I just wish we had more time together."

"I had an idea about that last night, actually," I said. "What if we made a Gabby-and-Teagan Date Night?"

"I'm listening," Teagan said, flipping her hair behind her shoulder.

"The same day every week," I continued, "or if that's too much, every other week or even once a month. We could always hang out more, but that way we'd always have our BFF time set aside."

"I love that!" She gave me a hug. "Thanks, Gabby."

"For what?"

"For . . . I don't know, really. Just being Gabby, I guess."

"You're welcome. And thank you for being Teagan, my BFF Forever And Ever."

"You mean your BFF . . . FAE?" Teagan giggled.

"Uh-huh. My BFF . . . FAE . . . AEAEAEAEAEAE—"

"Okay, I get it!!" Teagan said. She let out a big belly laugh and pushed me over on the bed. "Now, should we work on our poem? It's been a while."

"Definitely!" I said after I found my voice in all my laughter. Teagan grabbed her notebook off her desk.

"Oh shoot," I said. "I didn't bring my notebook."

"No problem," Teagan said, looping her arm in mine. "We're BFFs to infinity. You can share mine."

Time for Change

Friendship
By Teagan Harmon and Gabriela McBride

Gabby: Best friends are real
        a forever deal
Teagan: But that doesn't mean
        things can't change
        rearrange
Gabby: Sometimes be strange
Both: Between them

Teagan: I like coding
        and math
Gabby: I like to dance
        lead
        forge my own path

Teagan: This gives us a chance
        to try things on our own
        new projects
        new places
        and sometimes . . .
Gabby: New faces

To Infinity

Gabby: New friendships are formed
each unlike the last
new silliness
seriousness
Teagan: And what-happened-to-me?-ness

Teagan: I go back to the terms of the BFF deal
looking for something
that proves what I feel
is real—
that our BFF contract's been broken
It must be—
that new friend's not me
and can't you see how broken I am?

Teagan: But the BFF deal—
Gabby: Here's what it says:
The love between two BFFs
stays strong
through laughter and jokes . . .
Teagan: And even new friends

Time for Change

Teagan: The BFF deal—
Gabby: Here's what it says:
I promise I'll listen
with my ears, eyes, and heart
Teagan: And I'll have your back
if you stumble
trip, fall, or fail
I'll be there beside you
refusing to bail

Gabby: We're in this together
"we" and "us"
Teagan: You and me
BFFs forever and ever
Gabby: Always
Both: To infinity

Chapter 18

The Royal Dinner

S o?" Mama asked after picking me up from Teagan's house.

I nodded. "We're good. Better than good, actually."

"That's great, Gabby. I knew you two would work it out," Mama said. She smiled at me.

We were quiet for a few blocks. *One friend down,* I thought to myself. *One friend to go.* How was I going to make things up to Aaliyah for what I'd said the other day?

A few blocks later, Mama turned into the grocery store parking lot. "Ready to help me with some shopping? I was thinking enchiladas for dinner."

Suddenly, I had an idea.

"Can I invite Aaliyah and Isaiah over for dinner?"

Mama thought for a moment, then nodded. "Sure. Why not."

Time for Change

I shot off texts to Aaliyah and Isaiah as we headed into the store. By the time we checked out, they'd both replied *yes*. Isaiah was arriving at five forty-five and Aaliyah at six. Perfect.

Mama and I immediately started cooking when we got home. Red arrived when we were about halfway done, sweat dripping down his face. He must have been playing basketball with the guys. He said a quick hello, grabbed a sports drink from the fridge, then headed straight upstairs.

"Mama, can you watch the sauce for a minute? I need to talk to Red."

After she nodded, I bolted up the stairs. Red was just about to close his door when I stuck my foot in it.

"Red?"

I thought he might try to shut the door on me, but he just flopped down on his bed and took a long swig of his drink.

"I-I just wanted to let you know that Teagan and I mmm-made up, and we even wrote a new version of our poem for next www-weekend. I-I-I'm sorry we messed things up before."

"I'm glad to hear you worked things out," Red said, letting out a big breath. "I know the team will be glad to hear it, too. Everyone's really excited for next weekend."

"Yeah," I said. "And speaking of next weekend . . . I have some feedback I've been meaning to share with you."

"For my individual poem?" Red said, putting his drink on the floor.

I nodded.

"Hit me!" Red said bouncing up and down with energy he hadn't had a minute ago. "You know how I dig feedback!"

"All right," I said, laughing a little. "Have you thought about how you move during your performance?"

He frowned. "A little, I guess. Don't I move around?"

"You do," I said. "But maybe too much. There's not really a plan, is there? You just seem to walk whenever and wherever you feel like."

He laughed. "You know me, cuz. I like to let my legs flow with the verses."

"I know, but just hear me out," I began. "Do you have the words of your poem I can look at?" He quickly opened his poetry notebook and handed it to me. "Okay, remember how the Pink Poetics were stomping and stuff? Their movement accentuated their words. Like, right here, when you talk about Aunt Tonya being a soldier, what if you stood at attention and saluted?" I repeated the verse, standing tall and saluting on beat with the words.

He leaned back and rubbed his chin. "I like where you're headed with this, Gabby. Keep going."

"Awesome!" I said. "And if I help you with this, could you help me when Aaliyah comes over later?"

"Anything for my cuz," Red said. "Especially one who's my poetry sister."

Half an hour later, Isaiah arrived, and I filled him in on my plan for dinner.

Aaliyah rang our doorbell at six o'clock on the dot. But we were ready.

Red and Isaiah had tied sheets around their necks like kings' robes. Red opened the door, standing tall and regal, then bowed. "Hello, Your Highness."

I wished I'd had my phone so I could snap a picture of Aaliyah. The look on her face was priceless.

"Please, come in, my lady," Isaiah said, bowing, too.

As she entered, Daddy stepped from behind the door and quickly fastened my butterfly wings—I mean, my curtain—around her neck. "We are so pleased that you could join us this evening, Your Majesty. We have prepared a special meal just for you."

Aaliyah shot me a look that said *what is going on?!* I just raised my eyebrows. She'd find out soon enough.

It was Mama's turn now. She placed a crown made of

tinfoil on Aaliyah's head. "Only the best of jewels for our princess." Aaliyah giggled.

I giggled, too, but recovered quickly. My part required a certain decorum. I cleared my throat, then made a grand gesture with my arms. "Ladies and gentlemen . . . and cats," I said. Maya was watching from the coffee table. "May I present t-t-to you Her Royal Highness, Aaliyah Reade-Johnson, the Ever Enchanting Enchilada Princess!" We all bowed as Aaliyah stood there, giggling away. It was so hard to keep a straight face!

Maya, seemingly bored with our production, meowed at us as she ran upstairs.

And then Red started laughing, which made me laugh. Before we knew it, we were all laughing so hard we had tears in our eyes.

"Let's leave the princess and her lady for now," Mama said. "We'll meet you two in the dining room for our royal meal."

"Is dinner like this every weekend?" Aaliyah asked as we sat down on the couch.

"No," I said, between giggles. Then I composed myself as best I could, because I wanted Aaliyah to know I was serious about what I had to say next. "This is me-me tr-trying to apologize for wh-what I said the other d-d-day." I

did a quick check-in with my jaw like Mrs. Baxter taught me, tried to relax it, and started again. "I'm ssss-sorry for what I said. My friendship with Teagan is special, but so is ours."

Aaliyah nodded. "I think so, too. That's why it hurt so much when you implied that we weren't real friends."

"But I didn't mean it," I said. "We *are* real friends. Real friends have inside jokes." I gestured to my outfit and smiled at her. "Real friends help each other out, like you did when I needed to finish my costume. And real friends offer their honest opinions, which you're *really* good at."

Aaliyah laughed. "I'm just glad that I can be myself around you and not worry what you'll think," she said. "That's why *I* value our friendship so much."

"So we're good?"

She nodded. Then she opened her arms and hugged me. "And I'd even be happy to give you more honest feedback on your poetry, if you want. Starting with the positives first, of course."

I pulled back and beamed at her. "That would be great." Then I sniffed the air. "But maybe after the royal dinner. Those enchiladas smell delicious."

Chapter 19

Good-Bye for Now

In poetry on Monday, Red asked me to help everyone else be aware of their bodies during their poems, just like I had done with him. When we were done, everyone's poems were so much stronger. I couldn't wait for Land of the Free Verse to get up onstage on Saturday and wow the crowd—and the judges!

I grabbed my bag to head to ballet. This was going to be my last class, though Amelia didn't know that yet.

"Wait, Gabby!" Red shouted to me. He ran over. "We didn't get to your 'Dream Big' poem today!"

"That's okay," I said. "I actually have some revisions to do. Maybe you and I can work on it together at home later this week?"

Red nodded. "You bet."

"Amelia? Can I talk to you?" My heart was beating like a dozen ballerinas were doing grand jeté leaps on top of it. It was just me and Amelia in the studio now—the other girls had already left.

"Sure, Gabby," she said. "What's up? Great job in class today, by the way. Can't wait to see you rock those pointe shoes when we step away from the barre!"

"About that . . ." I started. The tiny ballerinas were doing petit allegro jumps on my heart now, faster and faster. I took a deep breath. "I-I-I've decided I'm not going to go en pointe. And . . . and . . . I'm g-g-going to step away from ballet completely, act-actually. Ffff-for now, at least." I couldn't read Amelia's face. Was she mad? "I-I-I know you really want me to go en pointe, but-but I-I-I . . ."

"Oh, Gabby," Amelia said. "Of course I want you to go en pointe, but only if that's what you want to do."

"I do," I said. "I mean, I did. May-May-Maybe I will in a few years." Amelia opened her mouth, but I kept talking. "I know it would be hard to c-c-come back later, but-but right now, I want to focus on mmm-my poetry."

Amelia give me a big hug as I breathed a sigh of relief.

"I'm so proud of you, Gabby," she said. "For following

Good-Bye for Now

your dreams, no matter what they are. You go be the best poet you can be. You'll always have a place at the barre if you want to come back, okay?"

I nodded. "Thanks for understanding." There was something else I wanted to ask Amelia, though. "Amelia? I was wondering if you'd help me with sss-something for my poem for this weekend."

"Of course," she said after I'd told her my idea. "I'd love to help."

She tapped me on the nose and headed out.

I picked up my bag to follow her, then stopped.

The sun had just about set, but a little light still flowed through the stained-glass windows high above me. I slipped on my ballet shoes and stepped into the square of red light at my favorite spot at the barre. With my heels together in first position, I slowly dipped into a plié, breathing out and then in as I went down and back up. Then I pushed my soles against the worn wooden floor, my tendus extending from red square of light to yellow square of light and back again. The entire world melted away until it was just me, the barre, and the dance floor.

I let my body—and my heart—say good-bye to the first Big Dream I'd ever had, and the first Big Dream I was letting go.

Chapter 20

Voices

Y ou two are going to wear a hole in the carpet if you keep pacing," Mama said to me and Red, a grin on her face.

We were all at McKenzie Middle School, the site for Voices. Once we'd checked in, a volunteer assigned us a private "green room" where we could sit before the competition began. It sounded really fancy until we learned that it was just a regular classroom. Bria, Alejandro, Teagan, and Isaiah had taken seats at the desks, but Red and I walked around, repeating our solos to ourselves. There were tiny tap dancers in my tummy again. I was nervous one minute and excited the next, especially since the only people who'd heard my revised poem were Amelia and Red.

Finally, the door creaked open and a woman wearing a headset peeked inside. "Land of the Free Verse? Time to go. We're about to start."

I grabbed Red's hand. Then Teagan came over and grabbed my other hand. Before I knew it, we'd all linked up in a tight circle. Even Mama.

"Guys, before we go," Isaiah said, "I just want to say—no matter what, I'm excited to be here with you all. It's . . ."

"AWESOME SAUCE!!!"

Mama jumped a little as we yelled, then laughed. "I like that. Maybe I'll use it in my classes."

The woman with the headset led us into the dark auditorium and pointed us toward a row of seats up front. The room was packed. Somewhere in there were Daddy, Mr. Harmon, Aaliyah, and Amelia, too.

"All right, poets!" the emcee said. It was the same woman, Jackie, from the high school slam. "Who here has been to a poetry slam before?"

This time, all six of us raised our hands.

Jackie warmed the audience up. As we leaned in and said "Mmm-hmm," the tapping in my belly was replaced with the same buzz I'd felt at the slam five weeks ago.

I glanced at Teagan. We were performing in Round One and were third, after two other groups. That meant there were only about ten minutes before we'd be onstage.

"We're going to rock this," she said.

I nodded. "We're going to blow their socks off."

The emcee gave a few more rules, then introduced the Sacrificial Poet. After her performance, the first team took the stage. They were really good, but also went over time, which—I can't lie—I was sort of glad about.

The entire auditorium was alive with mmm-hmms by the time the second group finished.

"Are you all ready for your next poets?" the emcee asked the audience. "Please welcome to the stage Gabriela McBride and Teagan Harmon from Land of the Free Verse!"

We walked to the center of the stage. The lights were harsher than the ones at Liberty, but I tried not to let them bother me. I took a few deep breaths. Beside me, I heard Teagan doing the same.

And then I began:

"B-B-Best friends are real,
a forever deal—"

Teagan took over, and just as I knew they would be, her words were strong and bold. I heard fingers snapping, and then shoes stomping. The audience liked our poem!

We walked to the sides of the stage like we practiced, then came back together for the end, the audience getting

louder and louder the longer our poem went on. We grabbed hands for the last few lines.

"You and me, BFFs forever and ever—" Teagan said.

"Always," I finished. Then together, we turned to the audience.

"To infinity."

We stood there a moment, soaking in all the applause. The spotlight didn't seem harsh anymore. It was as warm as the sun on a summer day.

Isaiah and Red performed in Round Two, knocking their poem out of the park. And then it was Round Three. Time for Red's poem about Aunt Tonya.

"Good luck, *bro*," I whispered to him as he stood up.

When he got into the spotlight, he said, "For my mom," then he stood there, not saying anything, just watching us. After a moment, he straightened himself to attention and launched into his poem.

> "Some see her as a pretty face,
> striking in her beauty.
> Some see her as a single mom,
> always and forever on duty.

Time for Change

Some see her as a doctor,
rocking multiple degrees.
Others see her as a soldier,
stationed overseas.
She's all of those things,
Captain Tonya Knight, MD.
But . . .

she's just 'Mama' to me."

There were some snaps after that line. Red continued:

"She taught me the simplest of lessons—
how to tie my shoes, brush my teeth.
But she also taught me how to think,
how to speak, how to seek
the knowledge that I need.
She won't let me be denied.
She is my mother, my mama—
the leader of my pride."

Red was doing great! He remembered to salute at the
right time, and even pretended to stalk like a lion on that
last line.

Voices

I quickly looked around. The audience was all leaning forward in their seats, just like they had during the Pink Poetics' performance.

"Before she left
to go overseas,
she kissed my forehead
and said to me:
'Be bold, my boy.
Be strong, don't fold.
Be sure, be steady,
and don't let your soul
be sold
the lies
of those that will hurt you,
hate you,
harm you
loathe you,
misuse you,
abuse you,
just because
you *are* you,
with your broad shoulders,
coarse hair,

black skin—
a jewel so rare.' "

Now people weren't just snapping their fingers and tapping their toes. They were straight-up cheering for Red. But he somehow began to speak louder, over all the noise.

" 'I will,' I promised,
and then she was on her way.
'I will,' I whispered,
as her airplane flew away.

So when I doubt, and worry,
and the path becomes hard to see,
I think of my mama, my captain,
and the man she wants me to be."

When Red finished, the entire room erupted. I mean, people were clapping and shouting and cheering and whooping and hollering and whistling and everything. I wanted to join them, but I didn't know if I could open my mouth and not start crying. My cousin truly had a gift for words.

Teagan caught my eye. I shook my head and wiped my tears. "That was so—"

"Amazing," Teagan said, finishing for me.

It took me the rest of Rounds Three and Four to compose myself. Were poetry slams always this intense?!

Get it together, Gabby, I told myself as the emcee introduced Round Five. *You're up next.*

Those tiny tappers were back in my tummy, and the ballet dancers were leaping on my heart again. This was it.

"Ladies and gentlemen, please put your hands together, once again, for Gabriela McBride from Land of the Free Verse!"

Teagan gave my hand a quick squeeze as I got up from my seat. I couldn't see her or anyone else once I was onstage, but I knew they were there, waiting to cheer me on.

I closed my eyes, made sure I was standing on both feet, and began.

> "The first t-t-time I put on ballet shoes,
> my mmm-mama says,
> I made everyone stop and listen.
> 'They're whispering,' I said,
> sliding my foot along the floor,
> 'Like you make me do in church,'"

I put my feet together in ballet first position and my arms in low fifth, creating an oval from my shoulders to

my hips. As I said the next stanza, I began a port de bras, moving my arms through a sequence of positions.

"Heels together, toes turned out—
the barre my pew,
the pliés my prayer.
And like any little girl
in a tutu and tights,
I dreamed of going en pointe."

I pressed my toes into the floor now, rising into relevé, my arms above my head in high fifth position. Then, as I said the next lines, I did some ballet steps.

"I www-wanted pointe shoes
like a seedling wants the sun.
I was patient,
persistent.
And my dream began to grow.
It burst forth into the sun!
But . . ."

I stopped dancing altogether.

Voices

"So did my voice."

I started hitting my torso and legs, like that boy had done in the high school slam.

"When I discovered poetry,
I discovered a beat,
a passion so pure
it was like its own prayer.
Ballet was church but this was—

I didn't know what it was
but it was legit,
like my soul had forgotten
what a whisper even was,
And yet . . ."

I stopped moving altogether and put my feet back in first position.

"There was a whisper inside me. It said:
That dream of going en pointe?
It's no longer the point of your dreams."

Time for Change

I snapped my feet together so my toes touched. Then I crouched down on the edge of the stage like I was smelling a flower.

"But these pretty petals of my pointed feet—
could I bear to uproot them now
when they were poised to bloom so soon?

I couldn't do it,
wouldn't do it,
until one day I realized—
there wasn't room in the garden
to grow two dreams at once."

I motioned like I was picking a flower from the stage beside me, then stood up.

"And so, today
I gently dig up my dream
of dancing on my toes.
I hold it right here, in front of my heart
and do a tendu or two—
a prayer for safe journeys ahead.
Then I gather all my bravest thoughts and blow."

Voices

I did a big exhale, like blowing a dandelion away.

"I watch as the seeds fly away with the
    breeze.
Who knows?
The wind could blow them back someday.
But for now, I clear my throat, I grab my pen.
I've got stanzas and verses to write!
I've said my good-byes
and they're all good because,
I'm surer than ever before—
if I have a dream that demands room
    to grow,
I also have the courage to let another one go."

I stood there for half a second, then bowed my head to show I was done.

There was a moment or two of silence, and then from somewhere, an "mmm-hmm!" broke the spell. The audience erupted with stomping, clapping, and hollering. Mama and Amelia were both smiling so big it looked like their faces might break.

Teagan wrapped me in a bear hug as soon as I got back to my seat.

"That was so great!" she whispered, wiping her eyes. "But you're giving up ballet? I can't believe it!"

I nodded. "I've got some other dreams that are more important to me—big ones and little ones," I said. "I'll tell you more later, okay?"

She nodded, and we turned our attention to the stage for the next poet.

"You were amazing!" Aaliyah said to me over the DJ's music after Round Five was complete. We had some time to kill while the judges finalized the scores.

"Thanks," I said. "I'm so glad you came." I gave her a big hug, then looked around. I wanted to reintroduce Aaliyah to Teagan, but Teagan had disappeared.

I spotted her at the rear of the auditorium, talking to a skinny kid I didn't recognize.

"Hey, you ran off," I said, when Aaliyah and I got back there.

"Oh, sorry," she said. She looked back at the boy. "I wanted to say hi to Aaron. We're friends from school. He's the one who made that drum program."

"Oh, cool!" I said, nodding at Aaron. Then I gave Teagan a look that said *you didn't tell me Aaron was coming!*

She replied with a look that said *you didn't tell me Aaliyah was coming!*

We both smiled.

A few minutes later, the music died down.

"It's time!" Teagan squealed. She grabbed my hand and squeezed hard.

"Time to not break my hand," I said, shaking it out and waving to Aaliyah and Aaron. "We'll see you guys later!"

Jackie called each group back to the stage, where our team linked up like we had before. Isaiah was right—win or lose, I was glad to be here with my friends—the poetry group, and Aaliyah. And Mama and Daddy, too. And even Teagan's new friend, Aaron. This was Little Dreams coming true.

But would my Big Dreams come true today?

The emcee took a clipboard from the scorekeeper. Behind us, the DJ played a drumroll loop. I squeezed my eyes shut.

"And third place goes to . . . Rhyme Time!"

A few feet away from us, one of the groups started jumping up and down and hugging each other. I let go of Teagan and Red's hands long enough to wipe the sweat from my palms. My stomach was all twisted up.

"Second place goes to . . . The McKenzie Mauraders!"

I hollered for the McKenzie team. Their awesome-sauce

performances had already given me so many ideas on how I could improve my own poems. But they were *really* good. Did that mean we hadn't—

"And first place goes to . . . Land of the Free Verse!"

I was sure I could hear Mama yelling all the way from her seat. Red thrust his fists in the air and started running around. I started jumping up and down with Teagan. Red and Bria did a little dance. And Isaiah started yelling, "I knew it! I knew it! Here we come, Pittsburgh!"

"And," Jackie continued, speaking over all our screams, "there are two special announcements I'd like to make." We all quieted down. "We'd like to recognize a poem that scored higher than any poem performed by a sixth grader in the history of this competition." She looked behind her. "Gabriela McBride, could you come up to the front?"

What?!

"Gabriela," Jackie said. "We've never seen a performance like that from a poet your age. Am I right, audience?"

All the snaps, stomps, and cheers proved she was. I beamed.

"We hope we see you—and your team—at many slams to come. We can't wait to see how your dream grows." She winked at me, then nodded to let me know I could return to my group.

Voices

"We'd like to recognize another outstanding poet," Jackie said as Teagan embraced me in a silent hug.

"This poet's performance scored a 9.8, which is the highest score we've ever had at this event," Jackie continued. "Red Knight, would you come forward?"

Red stood there, frozen, his mouth hanging open. I nudged him. "Did you hear that, Red? The emcee is calling you!"

He shook his head. "My poem scored the highest?" His eyes started tearing up. "But how . . . that's so . . ."

"For a lean, mean, flowing machine, you're really struggling with your words," I said. I pushed him again. "Now go up there."

But instead of walking to the front, Red took a second to wrap me in the biggest, bestest hug he'd ever given me.

"What about your rep?" I teased.

He shook his head. His face was wet with tears. "Thanks, Gabby. I wouldn't have scored like that without your help on the choreography, I'm sure of it. Thank you so, so, so much."

You know what?

It feels good to achieve your own Big Dreams.

But it feels just as good helping someone else achieve theirs.

"So, cuz," Red said to me in the car on the way home,

"you ready to show Pittsburgh how awesome Land of the Free Verse is?"

"You bet," I said.

Then I dug my DREAM BIG notebook out of my bag and turned to a brand-new page.

🤍 About the Author 🤍

Varian Johnson is the author of several novels, including *The Great Greene Heist*, which was an ALA Notable Children's Book, a *Kirkus Reviews* Best of 2014, and a Texas Library Association Lone Star List selection; *To Catch a Cheat*, which is another Jackson Greene adventure; and *Saving Maddie*. He lives with his wife and daughters near Austin, Texas.

🤍 Special Thanks 🤍

With gratitude to **Leana Barbosa**, M.S. CCC-SLP, for contributing her knowledge of speech therapies and language pathology; and **Sofia Snow**, Deputy Director at Urban Word NYC, for guiding Gabriela's poetic journey and contributing some poetry.

Parents, request a FREE catalogue at
americangirl.com/catalogue

Sign up at **americangirl.com/email**
to receive the latest news and exclusive offers

READY FOR ANOTHER
CURTAIN CALL?

Visit
americangirl.com
to learn more about Gabby's world!

A group of girls so close, they're just

Like Sisters

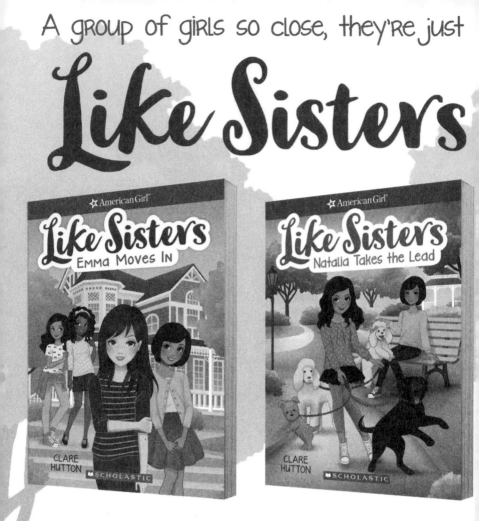

Emma loves visiting her twin cousins, Natalia and Zoe, so she's thrilled when her family moves to their town after living 3,000 miles away. Emma knows her life is about to change in a big way. And it will be more wonderful and challenging than any of the girls expect!

Several dogs are staying with their owners the family's B&B. Natalia eagerly volunteer to watch and walk all of them with the help her sister Zoe and her cousin Emma. But Z and Emma have their own commitments, a Natalia is quickly overwhelmed. When one the dogs goes missing, will Natalia be able step up and make things right?

★ American Girl
SCHOLASTIC